DATE DUE

JUL. 15 1993	NOV 4 1996	
AUG 24 1993	MAY 9 97	
NOV 8 93	MAR 17 99	
	AUG 10 '02	
MAY 23 1994	SEP 19 0,6	
JUN 23 1994		
AUG 26 1994		
MAR 24 1995		
APR 6 1995		
AUG 11 1995		
OCT 17 1995		
OCT 31 1995		
FEB 10 1996		

D1496213

DISCARDED

F
MAR
C

Martin, LaJoyce
The Other Side of Jordan

CASEY TOWNSHIP LIBRARY
CASEY, ILLINOIS 62420

DEMCO

The Other Side of
JORDAN

The Other Side of JORDAN

by LaJoyce Martin

36671

Casey Township Library
Casey Illinois 62420

The Other Side of Jordan

by LaJoyce Martin

©1992, Word Aflame Press
  Hazelwood, MO 63042-2299

Cover Design by Tim Agnew
Art by Art Kirchoff

All Scripture quotations in this book are from the King James Version of the Bible unless otherwise identified.

All rights reserved. No portion of this publication may be reproduced, stored in an electronic system, or transmitted in any form or by any means, electronic, mechanical, photocopy, recording or otherwise, without the prior permission of Word Aflame Press. Brief quotations may be used in literary reviews.

Printed in United States of America

Printed by

Library of Congress Cataloging-in-Publication Data

Martin, LaJoyce, 1937–
      The other side of Jordan / by LaJoyce Martin.
            p.   cm.
      ISBN 0-932581-98-6
      I. Title.
PS3563.A72486074   1992
813'.54—dc20   92-14091
                                                                        CIP

Casey Township Library
Casey Illinois 62420

MAR

To
"Mickey,"
the only cowboy
I ever loved

CONTENTS

CONTENTS

Chapter 1

THE CLOTHESLINE'S CUE

"Not *that* house!"

Jordan Thomas looked around to see who spoke the words—and was surprised to find that they came from his own mouth. *No, they came from his heart.*

"Are you trying to tell us where we can strike and where we can't?" Flynn's mordant smile matched his fermented breath and cold eyes. "Because if you *are* . . ." His hand patted an unfriendly gun at his side.

"No, I—"

"Then what's your problem?"

Jordan turned his face back toward the clothesline in the yard. *The dress.*

Memory called up last Saturday's drama and presented it in one grand replay. He saw himself sauntering down Main Street, past Boscoe's Hardware, headed for the saddle shop at the far end of the block.

A warning yell had stopped him in time to see the runaway horse bucking and snorting toward the boardwalk. A girl jumped back and stumbled. In the fall, she caught her dress on a railing and was held there. With one quick movement, he snatched her from the danger, tearing a great gash in her skirt. The animal's deadly hooves came down with a crack, leaving crescent scars on the walkway.

This secondhand scene, tattooed on his mind, showed her eyes just as trusting, her dimpled smile, her burning cheeks. "Oh, thank you, sir! The—the horse frightened me. I thought surely I would be trampled." She made no effort to release his arm. "I'm indebted to you."

He could still hear the soft Southern accent, the sweetly burred speech. He would have risked certain death for her at that moment.

"Much obliged, ma'am. But I'm sorry about your skirt."

"My skirt?" She looked down at the damage. "Oh! But it's better for the dress to be torn than *myself.*"

"A greater truth was never spoken."

"I'll say a prayer for you every night," she said. It gave him a strange, warm feeling that seemed to paralyze him. While his boots stayed, as if glued to the boards, she moved away.

In an effort to rouse his feet from their immobility, he glanced down. There where she had fallen lay a small silver object. He picked it up and turned it over in his clumsy hands. It was a tiny locket; it must have belonged to her. He tried to push his way past the deliberating shoppers to find her and return it, but she had vanished.

She said she would say a prayer for him. What had she meant?

The drama faded as visions will, and Jordan felt that same warm sensation now as he stared at her dress with its smile-shaped rip hanging on the clothesline.

"Well, are you going to speak up?" Flynn's moustache did a war dance. "Some of your kin live here?"

"No."

"Somebody you know?"

"Not by name." Jordan's mind fogged and cleared. "Look, Flynn. If you'll skip over this house and go to another, I'll give you my part of the take at the next place. It's a promise."

"You're going soft on us, boy."

"I don't think we'd find much here. And I don't want anyone—hurt."

Flynn took a threatening step toward Jordan. Anger bunched his jaw muscles.

Jordan's mind reached and grabbed, clouded again, cleared again. In the short time he had traveled with Flynn, his quick perception picked up on the tough man's one weakness. Superstition. He'd seen Flynn skirt graveyards with a wary eye and change directions to undo the "spell" of a black cat. Jordan bit into Flynn's Achilles' heel now.

"Do you see that clothesline, Flynn?"

"I'm not blind."

"Did you notice those three socks hung *upside down?* That's a bad sign. And notice that there are three socks, not two or four. They're not paired. That doubles the omen. And besides all that, two of them are black, and only one is white. The two black socks have the white one surrounded. That's two to one against you. I don't think you would want to walk past those three inverted socks to that house. I'd pity your poor soul if you did."

Flynn's eyes dilated. "You're telling me that there

11

might be a *stiff* in the parlor of that place?"

Jordan shrugged. "You never know what might be in the parlor."

Flynn spat. "I'm afraid you're going to be more trouble to us than you're worth, Thomas."

Jordan met his accusing glare with an assumed calmness. "I might be, and I might not be. Go ahead and try the house if you dare."

Flynn spun on his heels. "C'mon, boys. This is the only time we'll cotton to Thomas. If it happens again, he's out." He fingered the pistol once more for emphasis.

That night, Jordan tossed his bedroll into a terrible disorder. He was disturbed. He'd been with the outfit less than a month and was already disillusioned. Flynn, a dozen years his senior and the self-appointed leader of the outlaws, had little concern for human life—except his own. He'd painted a pastel-colored picture of simple looting for survival on the way to a good job on the West Coast. The promise of a job was what enticed Jordan to join the rovers. But Flynn's disrespect for women and children made Jordan sick inside. Flynn was no gentleman.

Less cruel, but putty in Flynn's hands, was a man named Pete. Jordan concluded that Pete might as well have been brain-dead for all the thinking he did on his own. He yessed all Flynn's decisions, good or bad, right or wrong. A ragged scar from his left eye to his chin sabotaged any good looks he might have once had. It was obvious he cared not a shard whether or not they ever made it to the West Coast. "I always been allergic to work, boss," he told Flynn, with a yellow-toothed grin. "My paw always said I had a heap more dirt on my tongue than on my hands."

The third man, dark-countenanced and moody, kept Jordan guessing. Whatever his real name, Flynn called him Lucky. Jordan suspected the man had a soft spot in the middle of him somewhere. He was kind to his horse and had even helped Jordan remove a splinter from his hand, wincing when Jordan winced. To say that he was friendly was a stretch of facts, though.

Snores rumbled from a nearby pallet. A falling star tailed a white streak across the black background of sky like chalk across a chalkboard, quickly erased. *Someday,* Jordan thought, *this part of my life will be behind me, blotted out.*

The innocent-faced girl said that she would say a prayer for him every night. Maybe she was saying that prayer now. . . .

How did one pray? Somewhere, just beyond rationalization, was the recall of a mother laying her hand on her baby's head and saying words. If the saga belonged to him, he had been too young to remember any details of it. His mother had died so long ago that any sentiment of a mother's love would have to be invented.

Of his father, Jordan knew nothing. His childhood suffered a series of pillar-to-post episodes that were not pleasant recalls. While still an unfinished adolescent, he vowed that as soon as he was old enough, he would burden no one with his care.

In his teenage years, he worked on odd jobs, never gaining enough to leave his locality for more lucrative employment. He failed to collect his wages on numerous occasions. The deadlock of reversals and setbacks wearied him.

CASEY TOWNSHIP LIBRARY
CASEY, ILLINOIS 62420

At a low moment in Jordan's life, Flynn and his cohorts came through the hamlet of Hoffman and took rooms at the boardinghouse where Jordan lodged. While Jordan ate his bowl of greasy soup, Flynn ordered the cook to prepare "steaks the size of saddle blankets" for him and his men. The roll of money he pulled from his pocket made an impression on Jordan. He had never seen so much cash.

When Flynn offered to take Jordan on with the promise of a future in the California gold mines, Jordan jumped at the chance. Fate had finally smiled upon him, he decided. This was his break.

"How old are you, kid?" Flynn had asked.

"I'll soon be a man, sir."

"But you're not quite there?"

"Two months shy."

"That's good news. In case you get into trouble, you won't be tried in the courts as an adult."

"I wouldn't be planning on getting into trouble, sir."

"None of us plan to get caught, *ever*." He snorted and it wasn't a pleasant sound. "But we sometimes get the rap for something we don't plan on or didn't do."

"I'd just be going along for the job in the mines."

"We have to survive between here and there. If we stop and work for our feed in every town, we'll be half a century on the trail. We might have to do a bit of low-key stealing. For food. Nobody begrudges a thief a loaf of bread. It's better than begging."

Fair enough, Jordan thought. But it hadn't turned out that way. At the first house they seized, Flynn demanded that Pete tie up an elderly gentleman. Jordan fought back a tight feeling that squeezed off his breath

14

when he saw the fear in the old man's eyes.

And they took more than biscuits; they took money and other valuables that the old man had probably spent a lifetime collecting. Jordan felt cheap and guilty. But still, they hadn't really harmed anyone. And maybe they got enough to get them on to their destination, where he would be able to make an honest living for himself.

The three men lived high and boisterously on the proceeds from the robbery. Flynn drank a great deal of whiskey, Pete mimed him, and Lucky bought a new saddle. Jordan saved his money. However, one morning when he awoke, it was missing.

"I seem to have lost my money somewhere," he told Flynn.

The crude man guffawed. "We've *all* lost our money somewhere, kiddo, so it's about time for us to pass the collection plate again, ain't it?"

Jordan felt disheartened; it had only been two weeks since their "low-key stealing" and they were already penniless. Worse yet, they had made no progress toward California and the work in the mines.

There was no one at home on their second raid. Or, if there was, they were in hiding. It fell Jordan's lot to guard the door. He stood on the front stoop, nervous and agitated. He never knew what went on inside the house, but Flynn came out with a wicked smirk on his face. He gave Jordan several dollars.

More revelry followed the second break-in. More drinking. And some gambling in town. Flynn lost most of his money to games, and Pete fell into the same ditch.

Jordan hid his stash this time. Eventually, he reasoned, he'd have enough saved for a stagecoach ticket to

California. Then he'd slip away and make the trip alone.

Today the raiders made their third forced entry. A big haul it was, and Jordan's part went to Flynn, as he had bargained. It would set him behind, but no cost was too great to save the girl who was saying prayers for him. As he saw it, he surely needed those prayers.

Jordan lay and pondered his predicament. The horse that he rode belonged to Flynn. Flynn owned the weapons and even the map. The unscrupulous man had him over a barrel. Soon, though, he would have enough to build a world of his own apart from these depraved men. He was not their kind; he didn't want to be their kind.

As he fell into a troubled half-sleep, he remembered the locket. The picture of an older woman in a hinged, heart-shaped frame bore a resemblance to the girl. Could it be her mother? An older sister? A cousin? The lady in the portrait looked much more well-heeled than the girl had appeared to be. But then, one could tell little about daguerreotypes.

How he would get the possession, obviously precious, back to the girl plagued his mind. But wait! The solution came to him now. He knew where she lived. He had seen her torn dress on the clothesline just today. He would return her keepsake to her! His heart gave a crazy leap.

What excuse would he use to get away from Flynn and Pete and Lucky? It wouldn't be an easy task. Flynn had taken to watching him like a hawk.

I must find a way, God. It was the closest thing to a prayer that Jordan Thomas had ever prayed in his life.

Chapter 2

LOCKET LOST

"One of your white socks didn't show up at the rub board yesterday, Maynard. Have you any idea where I might find it?"

"Why yes, Lydia." Mr. Matterhorn dropped his armload of split kindling into the firebox beside the cookstove. "I think it's probably somewhere down near the Capitol." Mischief played havoc with his straight face.

"You're joshing me!"

"Not at all."

"Why, Maynard, you haven't been to the Capitol in over a year—and that sock was in *last week's* wash."

"Yes, I know. Did you like the fish I caught for us?"

"The fish were wonderful. But don't go changing the subject."

"I'm not changing the subject."

"What does fishing have to do with that lost sock?"

"Everything. *Everything,* my love. I forgot my seine, so I used my sock to catch minnows for bait. When I got through fishing, I went to get my sock that I'd anchored

17

between two big rocks. In the getting—or the trying to get, I should say—the sock got away from me. Even now, it's probably swimming toward the ocean, minnows and all."

Lydia laughed. "It made for a funny sight, those two black socks and one white hanging on the clothesline."

"I don't expect anyone saw the comedy but yourself."

"I should hope not. I'd feel uncomfortable with anyone looking on my clothesline!" She lifted the lid of a heavy black pot to check on her chowder. "Well, it's no problem, Maynard. I have plenty of white worsted left. I'll just knit you another sock to replace the one you sent swimming down the river."

"You're not upset?"

"Oh, no. I enjoyed the fish too much to complain. Katie says we should send you fishing more often."

"Where is our Katie?"

"She's in her room mending the rent in the dress she wore to town last Saturday. That must have been a frightening experience for her—seeing a runaway horse coming directly toward her. But I'm glad someone was there to snatch her from beneath the animal's hooves. God has His angels posted anywhere we need them, doesn't He?"

"I'm sure He does, Lydia. But not all strangers are . . . angels. I'd rather you don't let Katie out by herself to pick berries or—or anything for a while."

Surprise and question arched Lydia's dark brows. "Why not? Katie is nearing twenty and has always been a responsible lass. She's perfectly trustworthy. I don't see what you are getting at."

"It's not that I distrust Katie. But there's . . . there's

18

been talk of some meanness going on in these parts. The sheriff told me that old Mr. Snyder's daughter found him tied up about three weeks back. The old fellow declared he'd been robbed by three men. They took most everything of value that he had. It frightened him so that he's been abed and doing poorly ever since. Being so nearly blind, he couldn't give a very good description of the robbers. There was a fourth man, he said, but that man didn't join in. He even came back to free Mr. Snyder, but the others caught him at the good deed and hauled him off with them."

"I'll caution Katie."

"I want *you* to stay in, too, Lydia. You're not to go anywhere unless I'm along. I'll pick the berries for you myself."

"It was probably just chance passers, Maynard."

"No. Greta Moore's house was hit a week or so ago. She saw them coming—four of them—and she hid. She grabbed the oilcloth from the table, wrapped it about herself and crawled back up under the harvest bench next to the wall. They never saw her, but then she couldn't see them, either. No one has been able to give enough information to identify them."

"Did they get Greta's valuables?"

"Everything they could find."

"How dreadful!"

"But the reason I'm cautioning you, Lydia, is that I found footprints just beyond the first tree row out back this morning. They were made by men's boots and there were several of them. Someone has been watching our place. And recently."

Lydia's hand fluttered to her throat. "I'm . . . I'm

scared, Maynard."

"Remember that we have angels encamped round about us, dear. Something or someone obviously frightened the intruders away. Anyhow, I'm staying close by in case those angels need human help. I have my shotgun loaded. Just please stay in the house."

"We've a host of strangers coming through since the opening of the West. And some of them are mighty sinful. Least ways, the gambling rooms are overcrowded."

"There will be some good among the bad."

"Yes, we have one good stranger to thank for saving our daughter's life. Oh, Maynard! We've already lost Benny and if we had lost our Katie, too . . ."

"Well, we didn't, love. Don't borrow trouble."

"Katie said the young man who rescued her from the horse was very kind. She was quite taken by his gentlemanly ways. I wish we could have thanked him personally. Katie didn't even get his name."

"He probably wouldn't want any special thanks. Most real gentlemen don't."

"Did Katie tell you she lost the locket my sister sent to her? Cynthia had it made especially for Katie. I'm sure she paid a dear price for it—"

"Where did Katie lose the locket?"

"She said she supposed she dropped it when she fell in town. She hasn't seen it since."

"Did she advertise for it? I can go . . ." Mr. Matterhorn stopped. "That is, both of you could go with me to town to look for it. I wouldn't leave you here alone."

"Katie went back and combed the area. When she couldn't find it, she left her name with several merchants. Somebody likely picked it up. With the crowd that was in town Saturday, we may never see it again."

"I hope Katie doesn't fault herself for the loss."

"It seems Katie is taking it badly. At least—*something* is bothering Katie. She's been quiet and withdrawn since Saturday."

"It isn't like her to fret over material possessions."

Frown lines drew a map on Lydia's forehead. "Before she lost the keepsake, she seemed excited about Ellis's coming for her. But she hasn't mentioned his name all week. I can't even get her to talk about the wedding."

"What would losing the gift from Cynthia have to do with Katie's wedding?"

"I've tried to figure it, Maynard. Perhaps Katie equates the losing of Cynthia's sterling piece with the losing of Ellis, since Cynthia is responsible for making the match." She threw up her hands. "It doesn't make sense."

"Don't let it upset you. Anyone who finds the locket will know that it belongs to our family. And any honest person would return it. The picture is identification enough. You and your sister look so much alike—"

"But that's where the resemblance ends." The twitch of a smile replaced Lydia's scowl. "We are as different as daylight and dark."

"Yes. You're the daylight and she's the dark. And that's one reason, Lydia, that I'm not comfortable with Cynthia choosing a husband for our Katie." Now he took up the worried look. "If she thought like you think—had your noble character—it wouldn't hit such a raw nerve with me that she would usurp our daughter's future."

"Maynard! She only wants the best for Katie!"

"Let me have my say, Lydia. I can forebear no longer.

21

I know that Cynthia was young when she lost her husband and Katie represents the daughter she never had but always wanted. But God gave Katie to us, not to Cynthia. Katie has grown up to be lovely and unselfish with what little we could provide for her. Cynthia's value system is not the same as ours."

"You are right, of course. Had we allowed it, Cynthia would have spoiled our daughter with her money. Even when we were children—my sister and I—she wanted the tangible things, I the intangible. She wanted purses and parasols and slippers while I wanted peace and happiness and love."

"So you see why I feel chafed of mind when I think of her influencing Katie in so important a decision as a lifetime companion."

"It is admirable of her to want a good life for her only niece. And she feels that Ellis Shelby is a perfect match for Katie."

Mr. Matterhorn took a deep, tired breath. "I hope she's right. Cynthia has always felt that you married below yourself when you married me, a lowly farmer. And she doesn't want Katie to make the same 'mistake.' If your sister had had her way, you would have wed a New York banker and lived in high style." The scabbed-over sore of bygone years festered again.

"But I didn't want to marry a New York banker! I wanted you. I married for love." She patted his shoulder. "And I've been happy. Cynthia can't understand me because Cynthia could never be happy without money."

"I want Katie to marry for love, too. How can she know if she loves this young man she has never met?"

"Oh, Cynthia assures Katie in her glowing letters that

she can't help but love Ellis. He's handsome, personable, and rich. That's more than we can say for any of the hometown boys. Most of them don't have *one* redeeming quality." Lydia sighed. "You've said yourself, Maynard, that we've had a crop failure among the local eligibles. Katie has already told us that there's no one here she would wish to marry. And she's marrying age. She'll be getting restless before long if we try to hold her."

"What's the old saying, Lydia? Better single still than wedded ill. . . ?"

"I think, Maynard, that you are just dreading to see Katie move so far away."

"Yes." The one bittersweet word incorporated Mr. Matterhorn's grief for his lost son and the anguish of parting with his only daughter. "We'll be so . . . alone, Lydia. And I'll never know what it's like to have a son-in-law because I don't *know* Ellis. I can never know him; he's not of my world."

"But surely you wouldn't deny Katie the chance for a better life. She'll have beautiful clothes, plenty of money, a large estate, a grand piano. . . . You know she's always yearned for music."

"I wouldn't deny her anything, Lydia. I'm a *father.*"

"We could move to New York to be near Katie. She'll have plenty of room for us."

"No." Mr. Matterhorn left no room for compromise. "I wouldn't want to leave Benny's grave. And besides, I'd never fit in New York. Cynthia would be ashamed of me—as she has always been."

Katie overheard the conversation and laid aside her mending. What would her life be like married to Ellis? To have servants and carriages . . . and a grand piano to

23

play all day long?

A feeling she could not identify sent a shiver through her chest and down her arms. Was it anticipation? Or was it dread?

Chapter 3

THE CALL

"Here we are, boys."

When Flynn led the men to the lopsided shack hidden in a grove of hackberry trees, he strutted like he'd found a castle. The apparatus, with its leaning add-ons, reminded Jordan of a woodpile that had fallen and sprawled.

"It looks vacant," suggested Jordan.

"It is, kid," Flynn said. "That's the whole idea. We'll be here for a few weeks and we need a roof over our heads. So I leased this place. It will look better on our part and sidetrack suspicion if we have a local residence. There's water here—" he gave his thumb a jerk to the left of the sagging porch. "Didn't take me long to find it. My grandpap was a witch wiggler and he taught me how to witch. Works every time."

"I ain't staying where there's a witch, boss." Pete started to back away, spreading his hands to form a shield in front of him.

"Don't be a blockhead, Pete. Witching is just a name for the way you find water," Flynn explained. "And in

25

case you ever need to know how to do it, you cut a green fork about three feet long off a tree and take one prong in each hand. Then you walk around holding the stick in front of you, right along the ground. The witch stick begins to wiggle and the main stem turns down when you get near water. If the water is real close, the stick pulls real hard. That's how I knew where the well was."

"Now ain't that something?" Pete grinned. "But if ever I held a dead stick and it started to move, I'd throw it down and *I'd* move."

Jordan was not amused. He faced Flynn with set lips; bitterness rankled in his voice. "What's the delay, Flynn? I thought we were headed for the West Coast."

"I don't have to have a reason for what I do," the man barked, losing patience. "But it happens that this time I do have a good motive behind my actions. We've got wind of some hidden gold about fifty miles north of here. It might be that we can make our fortunes without going all the way to the mines to do it. If we can get the same results without working, why work?" He slapped a hamlike hand against his knee and threw in a curse for good measure.

"Yep!" Pete mimicked the gesture. "Why work?"

"I'll just go on to California." Jordan met Flynn's inflamed eyes without flinching. "What I get, I will get honestly."

The leader rubbed the grip of his gun, slowly, deliberately. "Jordan Thomas, I'm thinking you won't go anywhere without the rest of us. We don't solo around here. Is that clear? Each of us knows a little too much about the rest of us."

"I'd never mention your name."

"That's what they all say until it advantages them to do so. I know that game."

Jordan stuffed his fist into his pocket to discourage the temptation to use it on Flynn's nose. His knuckles touched the locket. "When will we be heading north?"

"Today. We can't chance that much gold getting away from us."

"I can't go today. The saddle I'm using is in no shape for a trip. I'd planned on repairing it this evening. I won't be ready to travel until morning."

"This trip can't wait."

"I got an idee, Capt'n." Lucky's gravelly voice, seldom used, hung in the air, bringing them all to attention. "Why not let th' kid stay here an' guard over th' home place. We wouldn't want it to look like we'd up an' fled with all this crime talk a'ready brewin' 'round town. This kid ain't harnessed up for no big stuff like we gotta do, nowhow. He could put us all in danger an' crack up th' whole bust. Prob'ly ain't never fired a trusty-rusty in 'is life! 'Course I ain't sayin' it was a mistake to take him on, him bein' a minor an' all. I see yore point right clearly there." He paused and scratched his stubble of three-day-old whiskers. "An', too, that'd give us an extry horse to bring back our loot on if'n we left th' boy behind. Gold's heavy and we'll have a beaucoup of it."

"I'm not sure I trust the kid to stay here. You just heard him blubbering to go on to California."

Seeing his chance to find the girl and return her keepsake in their absence, Jordan spoke up. "I'll wait. How long do you think you'll be gone?"

"We're riding hard. Maybe two, three days. And if you're gone when we return," Flynn narrowed his eyes, "there'll be a mighty high bounty on your head."

"I'll be here when you get back."

"He's a man o' his word, Flynn," Lucky affirmed. "Ain't uprooted no dishonesty in 'im yet. I'll vouch for 'im myself. We can ride faster with only th' three of us."

Jordan's slight nod thanked Lucky. The mystery in the dark man's expression held an undecipherable message.

Within an hour, the trio was gone, taking all the horses with them.

Jordan's first thought was to strike out for the cottage on the outskirts of the village as soon as they thundered out of sight, but his better judgment checked him. They might come back on one pretense or another and find him slipping off. His ploy would be ruined. As hard as the wait, it would be better for him to delay until morning and be sure. . . .

Jordan went to bed early, grateful for the rare solitude. Cleansed of curses, the atmosphere seemed washed, unburdened. While he slept, hours that represented individual eternities ran their course.

A web of flannel-gray clouds hid the sun the next morning; the smell of perspiring earth filled the air. Jordan shaved, waxed his boots, and tamed his unruly hair into place with water before he put on his hat. Why he took such pains with his appearance, he could not have consciously told. His heart dictated his actions.

The distance to the girl's house covered, he figured, four or five miles. By horseback, it would have seemed a short distance, but afoot the miles crawled painfully slow beneath his boots. And not until the clothesline came into sight did he have any misgivings. He had rehearsed his speech over and over until it sounded like a recorded cylinder. "I found your locket, miss . . ." That would be simple enough. But what if she should question how he knew where she lived? He, who didn't even know her name? How could he explain about seeing her torn dress on the line without incriminating himself—and the others? *I just happened to be passing by and saw your dress.* It sounded preposterous. His steps slowed. He needed to plot something, some explanation. But then maybe she wouldn't ask; he hoped she wouldn't.

The atmosphere became heavier, holding its moisture with effort. The sky darkened. Jordan hurried, hoping to dispense with this obligation and get back to the old cabin before these clouds threw their rain-spitting tantrum.

Sprinkles kicked up the dust as he stepped onto the porch of the house. He knocked and waited.

The girl herself opened the door. There was the dimpled smile, the trusting eyes. She was just as lovely as the picture his memory had painted in the night. But scarcely were the first words of his memorized recital out of his mouth when a man hurried to her side, alarm in his eyes.

Jordan stammered apologies. "I'm sorry to bother you, ma'am. I found this . . . this . . . where you fell. I thought it might belong to you." He held out the heart-shaped token.

"My locket!" A glad light blazed up in the girl's violet eyes, and Jordan could not tell what brought the light. Himself or the locket? She took the silver heart with an expression of gratitude, but she was looking at him.

He turned to leave, his call complete. An inexplicable sadness mushroomed in his heart, for which he brought himself to task. What did he expect? He'd done a kind deed, but it was no more than any gentleman would have done. She owed him nothing. Her thanks was more than enough.

"Wait!" she called. "Please don't go yet. You must come in and meet my father." She linked her arm through Mr. Matterhorn's. "Father, this is the young man who saved my life." With a slight curtsy, she turned to Jordan. "And I'm sorry, sir, that I don't even know the name of my gallant rescuer!"

Jordan removed his hat but still stood on the porch. "Jordan Thomas, sir."

"And I'm Maynard Matterhorn." He stepped forward and extended his workworn hand. "Are you a stranger to our town?"

"Yes. I'm from a small place called Hoffman farther east. I'm on my way to California to work in the mines."

"Katie told us of your bravery—"

"Oh, it was nothing, sir. Really."

"Well, *we* think it was, her mother and I. Katie's all we have left, and if we'd lost her, I'd have her maw to bury, too."

Katie. What a lovely name. . . .

"And I'd be delighted for you to meet my mother, too, Mr. Thomas." Katie stepped back. "Please do come in. Our house isn't fancy, but we love guests."

Jordan found himself inside the parlor he had warned Flynn about. A smile teased his face. The parlor contained exactly what he thought it would—a beautiful young lady.

"I should explain why I came rushing to the door with my daughter," Mr. Matterhorn said. "There've been some crimes going on in our small community—a couple of robberies, an old man tied up, a lady badly frightened—and we're all a bit jittery. Since I found evidence that someone had been near our own place here, I've stuck pretty closely to my girls. When a man has a wife and daughter as precious as mine, he takes great care to protect them from harm."

"I understand, sir." Jordan dropped his eyes. "I would do the same."

Katie, who had gone for her mother, returned with the aproned woman. "Mother, this is Jordan Thomas, the young man I told you about. He has saved my life *twice* now! Once when he pulled me from the path of the mad horse, and now he has saved me from Aunt Cynthia's wrath by returning the lost locket!" She held up the memento.

"Why, bless you, son! Katie has been quite worried about her locket."

Every fantasy of a mother that Jordan had ever conjured up stood embodied in the woman before him. *And she'd called him son.* An overwhelming desire to hug Katie's mother seized him. He put his arms behind him.

Mrs. Matterhorn looked like the woman in the locket's portrait, but her face was softer, her eyes more alive. And she looked younger.

"Doesn't he remind you of our Benny, Lydia?"

Tears hid under Lydia's smile. "That he does, Maynard."

Behind his back, Jordan squeezed the brim of his hat into a tight roll. "I'm sure that's the greatest compliment you could bestow upon me."

"Coming from my parents, it is," Katie nodded. "I've never heard them say that about anyone else."

Jordan swallowed a lump that fought with his Adam's

31

apple. How did one dismiss himself? He had never felt so at home anywhere, but, of course, it was time to leave. And he would likely never see Katie again.

"Lydia, why don't you set an extra plate so that Jordan can join us for lunch? He might like some of your berry pie. Unless he has business elsewhere that would require his departure from our humble home." Mr. Matterhorn waited for Jordan's response while Katie's eyes begged that he accept the invitation.

"I wouldn't want to inconvenience you—"

"Inconvenience *us?*" Lydia cried. "Why, I was just telling my husband yesterday that God has His angels posted when and where we need them. A meal is small repayment for your kindness in saving our daughter's life."

Jordan grinned. "I know nothing about angels, Mrs. Matterhorn, but I'll think I'm in heaven eating a home-cooked meal!"

"I wish we had more of those wonderful fish you caught the other day, Maynard." Lydia burst into laughter. "My husband used his *sock* to seine minnows, Mr. Thomas, then let it get off down the river." She turned to the kitchen, chuckling.

By midday, the rain slobbered over the window sills in rivers, the cloudburst making Jordan's departure impossible. "You might as well enjoy your visit, son," Mr. Matterhorn suggested, excusing himself to a neglected chore. "If you get out in this, I'd have to rescue you from drowning."

Jordan found himself sitting in the parlor with Katie—alone. She had on the same dress he had seen on the clothesline, so well mended with meticulous stitching that one could hardly tell where the tear had once been.

Chapter 4

FRIDAY THE THIRTEENTH

An empty bottle and a raging thirst whetted Flynn's temper. Pete humored him; Lucky was sullen.

The rain slowed their progress. They lost the extra horse to a swollen river. Flynn screamed profane words at Pete for the careless loss when, indeed, it was his own fault. He had insisted on the inadvisable crossing.

An out-of-season norther reached its cold hands over into the May night and gripped the trio. Wet and cold, they huddled in a small cave that Flynn filled from top to bottom with oaths.

"Who told you about this boodle o' gold anyhow, Flynn?" hissed Lucky. "You ain't never told us nothin' that's got roots. I ain't keen on follerin' idle rumors around th' country."

"We have to check things out, Lucky," Pete defended.

"That's what I'm doin' *right now.*" Lucky's emphasis lay heavy on the last two words.

"Truth is," Flynn said, "I found out about this accidently-like while I was playing for money last Saturday night. The old boy I was up against was soused enough to spill out what little brains he had. I saw to that . . ."

"He got your money, though, didn't he?"

Flynn's face grew mottled. "The information I got was worth more than the money I lost."

"I say he didn't spill all his brains if he went home with your money in his pocket." Lucky didn't seem to care how much he ired Flynn.

Pete shot Lucky a warning look. "Back off, Lucky," he demanded. "Flynn's getting mad."

A deadly silence that asked to be toppled saturated the cave. No one made a move, and the tension gradually leaked away. "Now, Flynn, please go on with your story," Pete said calmly.

"This witless character that I was shooting dice with got to bragging about his kith and kin—all smart, handsome, and rich. All I had to do was keep him talking. I wanted to find out about the rich ones. Of course, that distracted my mind and I forgot to snap my fingers and say, 'Come seven, come eleven.' I rolled snake-up, the lowest and losingest numbers, on every toss. But I knew what I was doing. Sometimes you seem to be losing when you are really winning. A big win is worth a little loss.

"I mentioned that my outfit was headed for the mines and that loosed his besotted tongue. He said too much. Said his two brothers had headed up a group and went that direction a couple years back themselves. They got filthy rich. He got word that they've made their kill and are on their way back to Carolina with it. I don't rightly know if Carolina is a place or a woman . . ."

"It's a woman."

"No matter. Those men are right here in this territory

now, laid up for repairs on their wagons, with all that California booty. It's our business to lighten their load, don't you think?" He gave a cracked laugh. "We'd be doing them a favor. Wagons won't break if they aren't so heavy loaded."

"Our business and our pleasure," sanctioned Pete. "Doing favors!"

"An' you b'lieved that half-lit gambler's story?" mocked Lucky. "Why, my gran'ma could embroider better'n that! You mean, Flynn, that you've brung us out in this nasty weather an' we've lost our best horse on that kind o' storybook fiction? What kind of a leader are you anyhow?" Scorn and anger met on his tongue.

Flynn reached for his gun, but Pete grabbed his sleeve. "No, Flynn! Not in here!" It was almost a whisper. "You'll be sorry."

"You think I am an idiot." Flynn spat the words toward Lucky. "But I'm not the fool you take me for. I have a copy of the note from the man's brother giving directions to their hiding place." He patted his pocket. "It's right here. Now what do you think of my smarts?"

"You're a cracker-jack, Flynn!" Pete flattered, too quickly. "How did you manage that?"

"I just told some bedtime stories."

"Bedtime stories are my favorite. Tell us."

"I said what a coincidence that I was from his brother's part of the country. And furthermore, I said, my own brother-in-law was in that very caravan. I praised my good luck in hearing the news because I'd been trying to locate my brother-in-law for a month to get a message through to my *sweet little wife!*"

"Your sweet little *wife?*" Pete howled, holding his

35

sides. "Your *wife!* I've never heard a *prettier* story, Flynn. Why, that one would win a beauty contest."

"It worked, whatever its looks."

"Is that all you told him?" Pete egged him on.

Flynn spun more tales, weaving as he went. "Of course not! I said that my children would be so happy to hear from their daddy—that I just knew my little girl would cry her little eyes out for joy!"

"You didn't!"

"That one almost got me in a fine kettle of fish."

"How's that?"

"The gambler wanted to know my little girl's name."

Pete laughed the harder. "What'd you tell him, boss?"

"I'm used to inventions, so I said *Carolina.* That's the first thing that came to my mind. I didn't bat an eye when I said it."

"I wish I could have been there. I always did like to see a cat tangled up in pretty yarn."

"I promised him we'd see if we could help his brothers with their wagon repairs. Of course they won't even need a wagon when we get through. . . ."

"You know that tomorrow is Friday th' thirteenth, don't you, Flynn?" Lucky's words hit the walls and bounced back, making an echo in the cave. "An' Friday th' thirteenth is a *double* unlucky day when it comes in May. That date has been carved on many a tombstone. I wouldn't be surprised if half th' grave markers in th' world have that date on them." Playing on Flynn's superstition had worked for Jordan Thomas. It might work again.

Flynn cast a cautious look over his left shoulder.

Lucky tossed the twig he wallowed between his teeth

onto the embers of the campfire. "I've never knowed anybody to try anything new on a May-the-thirteenth Friday that didn't have double-bad luck."

"You're the handsomest of us. You woo Lady Luck for us."

"That ain't my line, Flynn. That's Jordan's line."

"Maybe we should have brought Thomas along just to keep the hexes off us, boss," Pete said. "Remember last Monday."

"Last Monday?"

"Yeah, when young Thomas steered us away from that house that was voodooed by the upside-down socks on the clothesline . . ."

"I'm still not sure Thomas wasn't trying to protect some interest of his own at that house." Flynn drew his brows down. "Maybe his bonnie lived there. If you'll recall, there was a girlie's dress on the line, too."

"I recall, boss."

"I give in because we couldn't take the risk of finding a corpse in there—or becoming one."

Now Pete scowled. "Seems that kid has quite a few interests of his own. It isn't like you to take on a babe still wet behind the ears—" He suddenly seemed to remember who he was challenging. "I mean, I'm sure you had good reasons for inviting Thomas to be a part of our rig," he backtracked.

"You'll see my reasons soon enough, Pete. If any one of us gets booked, we can always shift the blame to him. All our witnesses would agree against him. He hasn't the record behind him that we have."

"I don't think you're bein' fair to th' kid," Lucky said.

"Don't waste your sympathy. He didn't have to take

37

the risk if he hadn't wanted to. Nobody held a gun to his head."

"He thought he was goin' to a decent, honest job. And I heard you threaten him before we left—"

"Don't worry, Lucky." Pete yawned and stretched his short legs. "With a leader as foxy as ours, the infant is in safe hands. Flynn knows how to cover his tracks better than a panther wearing moccasins."

"We've lost a horse and it was the one Jordan rides," Lucky reminded.

"You're going to go out and steal another horse for us, Lucky." Flynn locked his fingers behind his head.

"I'm not goin' to steal a horse for nobody. They'd as lief hang a man for horse thievin' as murder in this neck of th' woods."

"You'll steal one if I say so." The words slapped.

"You're supposed to ask what color, Lucky." Pete nudged Lucky with his elbow and exaggeratedly cleared his throat.

Volcanic anger smoldered in Flynn's eyes. "What was that supposed to mean, Pete?" He clenched his fists. "Were you mocking me?"

"Oh, no sir! I meant nothing except . . . except that it's best to obey and not to argue with *authority.*"

"Partners—" Lucky massaged his chin slowly. "We can't afford to get tetchy on the eve o' such a dastardly day. We gotta stay easy-tongued an' careful-handed with each other if we want the lady to favor us."

"Lucky's right, Boss."

"We're all tired and we got us a hard ride ahead tomorrow. Th' big boss here needs rest. Y'all crawl back to th' back of th' cavern an' get some sleep. I'll stay near

38

th' front mouth an' keep a close watch on th' horses. We'd be mighty unlucky if somebody got our steeds. I'll call if I need either of you."

"Yep. Our nerves will be better when we get that gold and something to drink. Let's call it a day, Flynn, and leave the night to old Good Luck himself."

Flynn was already crawling to the back of the den.

Lucky bedded down near the opening, but when the first spear of daylight pierced through the cave's narrow aperture, he and his horse were gone. They did not return.

"You think he'll come back, boss?" Pete asked.

"No, I don't. And I'm glad he's gone."

"Why so?"

"I knew the minute he mentioned Friday the thirteenth that there would be some bad luck. I felt it in my bones, and when I looked over my left shoulder, I saw a shadow. I thought it might be death stalking one of us. Can't you see, Pete?"

"See what?"

"That Lucky's leaving is our bad luck and it's over with. It's time for our good luck now."

"Sure, boss!"

"The jinx is broken. You don't ever get two bad lucks, because two bad lucks right together would be the same as one good luck to evil spirits. That's the way it works. There has to be a good luck in between."

"Then why didn't the white sock on that clothesline between the two black ones break the spell?"

Flynn rubbed his head. "Let's see . . . Now you're confusing me, Pete. Don't do that. I can't afford to get all confused about haints here on Friday the thirteenth!"

"Never mind, boss. Our bad luck is over. That's all

that matters. But how will we make this raid without Lucky? It takes two to strike and one to watch."

"We'll look for somebody along the trail to hire temporary. And I hope it's somebody with a bottle of grog. I'm getting powerful thirsty. If we can find a jug, that'll be our good luck today."

"How far are we from where we're headed?"

Flynn consulted his map. "Not very far."

"I guess it'll be left up to me and you to fetch us another horse to get those pokes of gold home on."

"We can do it." Flynn winked. "No problems."

"Yeah, we can do it." Pete parroted the wink. "No problems."

Chapter 5

A TORN HEART

"Someone did a splendid job patching your dress, Miss Katie," Jordan made himself comfortable in the horsehair chair. "Was it you who mended it? One can hardly tell where it was ripped."

Katie blushed. "Yes. Mother taught me the small stitches."

"It would be wonderful if a torn heart could be mended so perfectly, wouldn't it?"

"Oh, but it can be, sir! God is a master tailor when it comes to hearts!"

"I regret to say that I haven't a very close acquaintance with Him. Not that I wouldn't like to know Him better; I have just never had anyone to instruct me. When you told me that you would pray for me each night, I was grateful, but I didn't know quite what you meant by prayer. How does one pray? Is it something that can be learned from studying a book, perhaps?"

"Why, I just kneel and talk to the Lord like He was my best friend—like I would talk to you. Every night before I go to sleep, I ask Him to keep me and guard me and let my soul be ready for heaven. Then I ask Him to do the same for all my loved ones. And I put you on the list!"

"Thank you. I . . . I need it very much."

"I guess I thought everyone knew how to pray. Your parents aren't . . . Christians?"

"I have no parents." After he said it, he wished he hadn't. Katie looked as though she would cry, and he couldn't bear that.

"Oh, I'm sorry!" she said. "And to think, I have such lovely parents and you have none at all."

"Yes, you have a lovely family."

"How long have your parents been—gone?"

"I never remember having them. I was told by the townfolk where I grew up that my mother was a righteous, God-fearing woman. I wish I could have kept her."

"She must have been good to produce such a noble son!" Katie's eyes dropped in embarrassment after the words were out.

"I—I hope that I can live up to your evaluation of me."

"Do you know that the prayers your mother prayed for you while she lived are bottled up in heaven now, and they still belong to you?" Her eyes met his again.

"They are? Then I trust I may always be worthy to possess them."

"You have no folks at all? Anywhere?"

"None that I know of."

"It seems that would be a lonely feeling."

"Sometimes it is, ma'am."

"You were never adopted by anyone?"

"No."

"Don't tell Father!" Her voice had a delightful musical lilt. "He'll try to adopt you yet—and then you'd never get to your job in California."

"It might be worth forfeiting a job in California to have such a father! However, with a dutiful daughter like yourself, your father probably doesn't even yearn for a son."

"He does, sir. You see, I had a brother who went on to be with the Lord three years ago. Father misses him sorely yet. Scarcely does a day go by but what he mentions Benny. And there's no one to carry on the Matterhorn name now. But God knows best, doesn't He?" Her eyes, wide and serious, pinned him to the worn chair with its antimacassar-covered arms.

"I'm—I'm sure He does."

"If there ever was a true Christian, Benny was one. We all thought he might be a parson or a missionary. He could say a lot of Bible verses by rote. He—he was thrown from a horse and hit his head against a tree. He lived a few days, but he never regained consciousness.

"That's why I'm so glad you saved my life. It wouldn't have seemed fair for my dear parents to lose *both* of their children in horse accidents. I don't believe they could have borne it."

"I'm glad I happened by."

"I am, too. But I don't think it was happenstance. Father says nothing is just *happen* in the life of a Christian. The Good Book says the steps of a righteous man are ordered of the Lord. And that means a woman, too. God had you right there to rescue me."

"I'd like to think that."

"Mother scolded me for not getting your name. How

is it that you knew where I lived?"

There it was! The question he had dreaded! Now it came unexpectedly, catching him disarmed.

"I—that is—I and the men I am traveling with—passed near here last Monday. That must have been wash day at your house because I saw the clothes pinned on the clothesline and I recognized your dress—the one you had on when the horse frightened you. The one you have on now."

"Then it was you and your friends who passed near our house!" Something eased in her face. "Father will be so relieved to know that it wasn't the robbers. With so many rumors of mischief going around town, he was afraid someone was trying to harm us."

Jordan looked down at the boots he'd tried to make presentable. He couldn't meet her eyes. "It pays to be cautious."

"Yes. I'll be glad when this scare is over. Mother won't even let me out of the house to pick berries!"

"I—I don't think you need worry anymore." He brushed by the touchy subject. "I was glad to learn where you lived so that I could return the locket. I thought it might be valuable—at least for sentimental reasons."

"Yes, the locket was sent to me by my Aunt Cynthia. She's my mother's sister who lives in New York. It holds her picture. She and my mother favor each other in looks, but they've led very different lives. Mother married for love and Aunt Cynthia married for money.

"Aunt Cynthia was widowed at a young age and was left quite wealthy. She never had any children of her own; I'm her only niece. Since I was a lass in pigtails, she's had great plans for my future." Katie's eyes shifted to the calendar on the wall. Each day of the month, up until today, was crossed off with a large X.

"Plans?"

Katie nodded.

"I hope you won't be leaving—"

"I'm afraid that I will." A cloud eclipsed the light that had been in her eyes.

"But why should you move to your aunt in New York when you have such caring parents here? If I had been blessed with such a family, I—" Something in her anguished look made Jordan fold his sentence in the middle and put it away.

"I am betrothed to be married."

Jordan felt as though a fist struck him and knocked the wind from his lungs. He tried to get his breath. *She was betrothed!*

She nodded toward the calendar. "I've been marking off the days until Ellis comes. Today is the thirteenth of May. He will be here by the end of June. That's just six weeks away. And I haven't even started stitching on my wedding dress."

"Oh, I'm detaining you!" He jumped up.

"No, no! There's not enough light to sew today. A wedding dress has to be just right. Anyway, you can't go yet; it's still raining outside. Please be seated."

Yes, and it's raining inside my heart, thought Jordan. *I found my ideal of a woman and lost her all within one week.* Her dimpled smile. Her violet eyes. These were things he'd never forget.

"I've been promised for a year." Her lips moved, but the music was gone from her voice.

Jordan wanted to listen to the details, but quelled an

urge to stop his ears so he couldn't hear that she belonged to someone else. Someone better than himself, of course. His foremost thought was to get away, to excuse himself. Yet he had eaten from her table, and he sat in her parlor, so propriety demanded that he show an interest in what interested her.

"Aunt Cynthia has had Ellis picked out for me since I was a wee girl studying my first primer. I've never met Ellis myself—"

"You've not met the man you plan to marry?" His voice seemed to rise a whole octave in the course of the single question.

"No, but Aunt Cynthia says he would be any girl's dream come true. He's educated, handsome, and very wealthy. At least that is Aunt Cynthia's evaluation of him. And she knows what it's like to live a plushy life.

"I can't even imagine what it will be like to have servants and a real silk parasol and a tea garden all my own. Why, I won't know how to act!" She tried on a smile that fit poorly. "But Aunt Cynthia says she'll teach me. I've lots to learn."

"I rather like you like you are."

"You sound like my father."

"Do you love this man, Miss Katie?"

Katie bunched her small shoulders, an unladylike habit that she had never broken. "How should I know? Aunt Cynthia says that I shall, of course. He's coming in a lovely carriage for me. Mother says that the whole town will sit up and take notice.

"It's almost like a fairy tale, isn't it?" She clasped and unclasped her hands. "I've done a lot of talking to myself. I've told myself that I've never seen Jesus, either,

46

but I love Him. He's coming for me someday. I've sort of used spiritual matters to keep down my natural fears. Does that make sense?''

"I can't see any sense in it." His voice was almost edgy.

"I pray about my future every night when I pray for my friends and my family—and you. I don't feel exactly comfortable with the thought of going away with someone I've not met, but when he gets here, I'm sure I'll feel differently.''

"Promise me you'll be sure before you go away with him." *Why had he said that?*

"Oh, I think God wouldn't let me do something I'm not supposed to do. Don't you agree?''

Jordan made no response.

"The main thing is if he's a Christian. But surely Aunt Cynthia wouldn't match me up with someone who isn't. Ellis hasn't actually said in his letters what his convictions are.''

Jordan squirmed. This Ellis, whoever he was, should come clean with Katie. Although he couldn't lay claim to being a Christian himself, he did plan to find out more about it.

"Are your mother and father happy about—about someone else choosing your husband for you?'' he asked.

"Mother sees this as a great opportunity for me. I've always wanted to study music. There I'll have a grand piano, a tutor, and many fine concerts to attend. I think Mother just wants me to be happy. She says I'm at an age to think about marriage; I shouldn't wish to be a spinster. There is—'' she stopped and corrected herself. "There *was* no one here to call for my hand.''

47

Jordan pretended not to notice the correction. "And what does your father say?"

"Father," she paused and her voice broke, "doesn't want me to go away. He'll miss me so!"

"And so will I." He said it under his breath, but when he looked up, he knew she'd heard.

He turned his face away as a shovel of discouragement dug the grave for his dying hopes.

Chapter 6

THE CONVINCING PORTRAIT

Ellis Shelby dropped his arm onto the table. The diamond stud pin that held his cuff, a gift from Madam Goldstein, clicked against the marble top.

Cynthia misinterpreted the look on his face.

"I know you're worried sick, Ellis," she said, toying with a bronze letter opener that lay within her reach. "And I am, too. The sooner we get Katie out of that God-forsaken territory, the better."

"Mmmmm." Ellis was only half listening.

"These robberies and muggings and outlaw gangs—! It's ridiculous! I suppose I'll never understand why my sister chose to marry a rebel who would take her to such a primitive place."

"I've been thinking, Goldie—"

"Have you heard from Katie recently?"

"Yesterday."

"Did she tell you about the old neighbor man—I believe she called him Mr. Snyder—who was tied hand and foot and robbed?"

"She mentioned it, but I skipped over the details. When she starts in about her heathen land, I refuse to read it. Things like that are for the stage. I'm not interested in savagery in real life." He drummed his thin, white fingers on the tabletop.

"I'm frightened for Katie. So many strangers are traipsing through the territory to settle the West. Who knows but that one might kidnap her and take her along? I'm glad you'll be going for her so soon. In fact, I was just working on an announcement for the newspaper when you came. How does this sound?" She unfolded an ivory-tinted parchment and read the proclamation of a grand ball to be given in the newlyweds' honor in July.

"That's more than two months away, Goldie. Why bother to advertise it so early?"

"With society, my dear Ellis, the earlier one gets exposure, the better."

"I should prefer that we wait—"

She rushed on as though he'd said nothing. "That way, one gets the advantages of more publicity. Everyone in the upper circles wants to know what goes on in the private lives of important figures like the mayor's family. We've guarded this secret for almost a year, you and I. We wouldn't wish the news to leak out ahead of our announcement."

"I'm not sure I wish it advertised at all. What if Katie should back out at the last moment? Think of the embarrassment . . ."

"Katie won't back out. When a Matterhorn gives their word, they would die before they would suffer the dishonor of breaking a promise. And Katie has given you her word that she will marry you, has she not?"

"Yes." His sigh suggested the boredom of a child who is tired of a toy and wants a new one. "But are you quite sure she is going to fit up here in our fast-paced culture? A girl from outlaw country?"

"She'll adapt wonderfully fast! Katie has a quick mind. Madam Tuttle from the finishing school has offered to give her the polishing touches on etiquette that she needs. For a price, of course."

"In her letters, Katie seems miserably old-fashioned."

"You must remember, Ellis, that she has never been exposed to the world of refinement. It will be your pristine pleasure to introduce her to our way of life."

"I'm afraid she's too religious, too hidebound, for our lifestyle."

"All she has ever known is a clapboard church and a stodgy preacher. So what else could she write about in her letters? Religion and outlaws. That's all she knows. There's absolutely no social life in the territory."

"I wouldn't want someone trying to turn me into a goody-goody."

Cynthia rang for the maid and ordered spiced cider and frosted cakes. "I'm sure you'll please Katie just fine."

"I hope she lays down enough of her religion to please me."

"Don't be peeved, Ellis. She will certainly do whatever it takes to please you. And as to the ceremony, I would suggest that you have a simple service there. Just enough to satisfy Lydia and Maynard. Save the big celebrating for here. My sister and her husband might not understand our methods of rejoicing."

"Have they even a hotel where I may lodge in that antediluvian place?"

51

"Yes, certainly. There are facilities." She laughed. "Such as they are. You will think them crude in comparison to ours. And please do overlook Lydia's pitiful house. It's so small that the whole of it would fit twice in my ballroom. And do be careful of the outlaws, Ellis. People with money are a prime target for them."

"I'm not worried about outlaws."

"Lydia says that Katie is stitching her own dress, but I shudder to think what sort of frumpy creation it might be, so I am purchasing her a wedding gown and sending it along with you. It's to be a surprise, my wedding gift to her. I found it at the Silver Boutique and couldn't resist it. It was exorbitantly overpriced, but it's quite fashionable. It will show her lovely shoulders."

Ellis wasn't paying attention.

"You see, Ellis, I begged Lydia years ago to share Katie with me. I longed to give her ballet lessons, skating lessons, music lessons, the arts. I told Lydia we had the best schools in the world right here in New York. I do think I might have convinced her had it not been for Maynard. He's such a stick in the mud! I cried for a whole month when Lydia married him. He wasn't her type at all. Would you believe the banker's son wanted to marry her?"

"Josef Hasselbein?"

"Yes! But she said she didn't love Josef. She feigned love for a hapless youth she met down at the waterfront docks where she went to feed the seagulls. Such an incorrigible girl, that Lydia!

"Well, as I was saying, I knew there wasn't a ghost of a chance of my getting Katie after Maynard lost his son in that senseless horse accident. But I determined not to allow my only niece to spend the rest of her life as a ragamuffin in some heathen government territory that makes its own laws and resists modernization! I just can't let that happen to her, Ellis!''

Ellis stretched. "Of course not, Goldie."

"Well, if this write-up suits you, I'll get it to the society editor." She patted the expensive stationery.

"I really would rather wait another few days, please."

"Why, Ellis, whatever for? You will be leaving presently to claim Katie. We're past the deadline for turning this in now. I'm surprised we've kept the secret. Your counterparts should have suspicioned something when you started turning down engagements with other young ladies."

He shifted, coughed. "Well, to be truthful, I—I'm thinking about postponing the marriage for another year."

"Another year?"

"We're both young yet. Another year could only bring us more maturity."

"But, Ellis, we need to get Katie while she's young so we can begin training her in the social graces. At her age, who knows what notions she might take? What if someone else should show up in that year and attempt to steal her hand from you? And consider the outlaws. Have you thought of the risks of such a postponement?"

"No, but I want to travel abroad before I take a wife and settle down. To Australia maybe. Or to Europe. And I want to see France, too."

"Ideal! You can go to any—or all—of those places on your honeymoon. I'll finance the trip myself. International travel would be just the thing for Katie. It would remove her from the scrutiny of the town gossips, break ties with her backwoods family. We'll make it through this one introductory ball just so our friends can meet her and know that you are truly married. Then you'll wisk her off in a shroud of mystery. What a wise young man you are to think of traveling abroad with Katie!"

"I'm not sure—"

"Of course you are! All prospective grooms feel moments of apprehension. Katie will be so lovely that you'll be the envy of every young eligible in New York. They'll wonder where on earth you got this winsome doll and why they didn't discover her first! You'll have them standing in line to dance with your wife at my ball!" She threw back her head and laughed. "Ah, Ellis, just you wait and see! I'm hiring a private seamstress to make her a whole wardrobe of ball gowns. Lydia says her eyes are a beautiful violet. Even as a child, her eyes were her most striking feature. That means she will be a charmer in a gown of any color."

"I'm having second thoughts about marrying a girl I've never seen. Please don't be offended at me for my introspection, Goldie, but all I have to go on is your word about your niece. And sometimes older people don't see things as the younger generation does. What if I get to that forsaken land and find that Katie isn't at all as beautiful as you have portrayed her to be? You see, my dear lady, I like to *see* what I'm getting. And there are plenty of young ladies here . . ."

Cynthia reached across the marble table and caught his slim hand. "My dear, dear Ellis! You will find just the opposite to be true. Katie will be so much more gorgeous than you imagined that you will wonder that you were able to talk such a flawless creature into marrying *you!* Why, Ellis, when she was but a babe, a calendar company wanted her portrait for its advertisement. The president declared her the prettiest child he had ever seen. But Maynard—small-minded Maynard—would not let the company photograph her for public display. He thought it vulgar. That shows you how Maynard thinks." She made a face.

Ellis said nothing.

"And so you will give your approval for the announcement?"

Ellis bit his lower lip stubbornly. He hadn't touched his cider or his teacake. "I—"

"Oh, there is the post now." Cynthia pointed out the drape-framed window toward the road. "Will you run down and get my mail, please?" She needed time to regroup her thoughts, gather more ammunition.

Ellis hurried from the room, leaving Cynthia pestered with a dark brown thought. Had Beverly Judson been talking to Ellis again? That buzzard of society had picked away at the fiber of Ellis's affections for many years, and Ellis had a weak will. Even now Ellis was trying to back out on the arranged marriage. She couldn't let that happen!

Cynthia was worried. She would never let her vast wealth go to any pig-raising grub or gun-slinging outlaw that Katie might choose to marry if Ellis withdrew his proposal. Could she hold him to the marriage by law?

She took the mail that Ellis handed her. He tried to slide away, but she detained him. "Wait! Here is a parcel from my sister, Lydia. Let's see what it might be."

Ellis lowered himself back into the polished mahogany chair, keeping an eye on the exit while Cynthia pulled the trappings from the package. Her fingers shook as she lifted the picture from between two squares of stiff leather.

"Oh, Ellis! Look!" she cried. "Here she is! This is your Katie! I asked Lydia to have a portrait made of her for the tabloids, but I really didn't expect it to come this soon." She held the picture up proudly. "Now what do you think?"

The young man's eyes explored the pose for a long while. Then he gave a bold whistle through his front teeth. "Goldie, she's—she's everything you promised. I think I could marry her for her beauty alone! And what a shape!"

"Now you're talking sense."

He gave a coltish laugh. "Won't she wag the tongues of these New Yorkers?"

"Won't she, though?"

He jumped up and gave Cynthia an impulsive hug. "I can't wait to go for her, Goldie! By all means, put the notice in the paper. Get the news out. You have my permission to write anything you wish from this moment forward."

Ellis wolfed down the refreshments and prepared to leave. "I could feast my eyes on that face all day, Goldie, but I'm running late for a game. Please excuse me."

When he was gone, Cynthia sat talking to the portrait like a simpleton. "You did it, Katie! You won him over with the good looks from the *Irish* side of the family!"

Chapter 7

THE CRIME

"We got ourselves a fine piece of horseflesh, Pete." Flynn patted the rump of the big, black stallion. "He'll travel."

"I'm worried, boss. I hope I put enough whammy on the old man's head that he don't live to tattle. It frights me that he'd be able to identify me. With this scar on my face, I'd be live posse bait. The old fellow dodged and the first blow almost missed. Got him across the cheek. The second blow should have done it, though. But he was mumbling and moaning when I left. I'm afraid he was coming to his senses."

"He was off the path and nobody will ever find him, Pete. He'll die before he can get to help. He looked finished off to me."

"Maybe we shouldn't have tried to replace a horse on an unlucky day."

"Don't worry and don't guilt yourself. One man's bad luck is another man's good luck."

"I got a rabbit's foot in my pocket, boss. Do you think

57

that'll protect me?"

"Protect you from what?"

"The law."

"Lucky said rabbits' feet play dead and don't work on unlucky days."

"Can't trust Lucky. Lucky is looking out for number one. You know what I've been thinking?"

"You had a think?"

"A crack one. I'm figuring Lucky took off early this morning ahead of us trying to beat us to the location of that gold. What do you say?"

"Pete! You should use your thinker more often. Of course, you're right. That's exactly what he did!"

"And now that we mugged that traveling man and got his beautiful beast—that being our good luck—we may find our bad luck is that Lucky has taken the gold for himself and fled with it."

"Right again!" Flynn looked woebegone. "And you know what he'll do, don't you?"

"No, boss. My thinker don't reach very far into the future."

"He'll go back to the home place and get Jordan Thomas, and the two of them will go on to California without us. Don't you remember him saying he would vouchsafe for the boy? He gave the kid a peculiar look when he said it, too. There was something between the two of them."

"I recall it face to face, boss. But Thomas promised on a stack of Bibles he'd be there when we got back from this job."

"I never met a man that wouldn't lie to tip the scales his way."

"Naw, I guess not."

"But write it down, Pete. When I find those two double-crossers, I'll bore a hole in them that this pretty horse could walk through."

"I can't write, boss."

The more they talked, the angrier Flynn became. "Maybe we should start out to find the turncoats right now."

"Lucky has a headstart on us. We don't know when he left; he might have got the gold last night."

"I don't see much use in going on if the gold isn't there."

"We might be wrong."

"No, we're not wrong."

"Maybe Lucky didn't get all the gold. He only had one horse to haul with. The gambler told you his brothers made a big fortune. Could be that Lucky couldn't tote it all."

"You're getting mighty thoughty, Pete. There might be gold left."

"I didn't take Lucky for a traitor, did you?"

"He was always too quiet. I hate tight-lippers."

"We'll have to be more careful in picking our cronies from now on."

"Yep. And Friday the thirteenth is no day to be choosing a business partner. It might turn out to be an unlucky choice."

"Meaning the two of us will have to get whatever gold we can by ourselves?"

"We knocked off the old man and got the horse by ourselves, didn't we?"

"Yes, but he was traveling alone. There's no telling

how many six-shooters will be camped with the gold."

"If Lucky can get himself some gold single-handed, we can do it double-handed."

"If Thomas is gone when we get back, are you going to try to replace him?"

"No. He's no good to us anymore. The only reason I kept him is because he knew too much. He birthdays in just a few days and he'll be an adult by law, tried in any court just like us. Anyhow, he was too soft. Softies can't do anything but give away our game plans. The next man we take on will have to be big enough to take a bottle. Jordan won't have anything to do with drink." Flynn pulled the worn note from his pocket, tracing along his scribbled directions with a dirty finger. "We're on it, Pete. Let's draw straws to see who goes to the door. That's the only fair way."

Flynn held the straws, which accounted for Pete's drawing the short one. "It's your go, Pete."

Pete knocked at the door of the dugout while Flynn stood back with his fingers curled around the trigger of his gun. A skeletal man answered the knock.

"Has there been a dark-skinned man about twice a yardstick tall and riding on a bay come by here, mister?"

"No, sir." His words slopped out. "Ain't seen him ner nobody in the last coupla days. Can I holp more?"

"You might could." Flynn eased in close. "We've heard tell that you've got more gold here than you can handle, and we thought we might help you handle it."

"You've heard mistaken." The man kept his eyes on Flynn's gun. "Ain't no gold here."

"Someone relieved you of it already?"

"Never was none here."

"You're lying."

"You're welcome to have a look-see."

"You one of Gambler Bill's brothers?"

"No. They done gone on to Caroliney. Left last Saterday. A week gone tomorrow. I warn't feeling s'well, so I stayed on here until they backwards through."

"When will they be coming back through?"

"Can't perdict. However long it takes to get there and get the wimmen loaded I reckon."

"Friday the thirteenth, boss," muttered Pete. "Bad luck."

"Shut up, Pete!" Flynn turned back to the gap-toothed man. "Did they take all their gold on to this Carolina woman?"

"They ain't traveling with gold, sir. That's too risky. Most people with too much gold get lead poisoning from a bullet. You know the saying of the West: It's one thing to get gold but it's another thing to get home with it. They didn't try. Put all they had in the bank in San Fran. They've gone for the rest of their clan and are shunting them all to the West Coast to be nearby their gold. I'm afraid if it's gold you're after, you'll have to rob the San Fran bank to fetch it."

"You have none?"

"I left mine in the bank, too." His face was honest. "Didn't have much."

"Plenty of gold out there?"

"I'd be lying if I said there was. Truth is, the gold is all petered out. There's a lot of folks coming back this direction mighty disappointed. And clean busted. Someone hollered wolf too loud. We just happened to hit a virgin place and got in on the tail end of the run about two years back. Took us all this time to get what we did. Hard work, too.''

"I'm not hankering for hard work, boss," reminded Pete.

"Wouldn't be worth a fellow's trip out there?" Flynn asked.

"Not now, less'n you're in the bank-robbing business. Banks are full, but security's pretty tight."

"You sure you're truthing us that there's been nobody by earlier today who's already lifted your nuggets?"

"Do you see any tracks? It rained last night."

Flynn and Pete looked around. There were no tracks except their own.

"Fine horse there." The man nodded toward the saddle-ready stallion. "An extra?"

"Yep."

"Interested in doing some trading for a wagon?"

"Just bought him today," Flynn returned. "Gave a pretty price for him, too. You don't find ponies like this for sale every day. You'll notice he has a white stocking on the near hind leg. That's good luck. And the white don't come up too high, or else he'd stumble if it did. We're taking him back to a young man in our outfit."

"That is, if the boy's still there when we get back," Pete threaded in.

"Come in for some coffee?" the man offered.

"You don't have anything stronger than coffee?" Flynn asked.

"Coffee's strong enough for me."

Pete led the way into the earth house. "You had any bad luck today, mister?"

"Nary a bit."

"We've had some bad luck and some good luck," Pete told him. "A man left our outfit with one of our best horses this morning. That was our bad luck. Then we had good luck when we sto—, er, *bought* this horse. Then we had bad luck here. Now it's time for another good break. Boss here says there can't be two bad lucks in a row on an unlucky day because that would be the same to the haints as a good luck. I can't keep it all straight."

"If you're talkin' gold, the only good luck I've heared about is up Colorado way."

"Colorado, you say?"

"Yep. They found it there and there's a heap more of it than there was in Californy. It's a mite harder to come by, they say, but those Colorado hills are *flowing* with it. There's many a year's worth of digging."

"Let's head for Colorado, boss."

"We might bargain in the horse for payment if you'd like to go along with us and show us where the gold is, mister."

The man held up a gnarled hand. "It's a temptation, but I ain't up to the trip. I got a leg busted on this trip, and I ain't been worth a Confederate dollar since. That's why I'm here."

"Wouldn't want him anyhow, Flynn," Pete kicked Flynn under the table with the toe of his boot. "He don't drink nothing stronger than coffee."

The day was waning when the two men and three horses left the dugout empty-handed.

"What you think, boss?"

"We win some, we lose some."

They rode in silence until Pete shouted, "Look!" He pointed toward a conglomeration of pots and barrels hidden in the underbrush. "A still!"

"It can't be, Pete. That would be two good lucks in a row."

"No it wouldn't."

"Yes it would."

"Let's count it up, boss. Lucky left us. That was bad luck number one. Then we got the stallion. That was good luck number one. After that we didn't find any gold. That was bad luck number two. Next the man told us about the Colorado mines, and that was good luck number two. Now . . ."

"See. It's time for bad luck."

"What did you say about two lucks of the same kind in a row?"

"Stop flapping your jaws and let's get to this still so I can quench my thirst!" Flynn dismounted on the run.

Pete panted up behind him. "Too good to be true, isn't it, boss? Whiskey!"

Flynn bent over, straightened up. "There's no whiskey here, Pete. This place has been abandoned."

"Scared off by revenuers, I guess. That's the worst bad luck we've had all day."

Flynn kicked a rock and sent it flying toward Pete. "I'm sick of any luck, good or bad! I'll be glad when this lousy day is over."

Pete dodged the rock. "Me, too," he echoed. "I'll be glad when this lousy day is over."

"If you're going to repeat, Pete, you have to say it seven times."

"Me too. Me too. Me too. Me too. Me too. Me too. Me too." He counted on his fingers.

Flynn laughed at him, an unpredictable and mirthless laugh.

They rode into the night. A new moon decorated the clear sky. When Flynn saw the moon, he snatched his leather pouch from his pocket and turned it over in his hand.

"Why did you take out your purse, boss?"

"If you turn your purse the first time you see a new moon, then your money will double in the moon's cycle."

Pete chuckled, taking a risk of agitating Flynn. "Nothing doubled is still nothing, boss!"

Chapter 8

THE DECISION

I *must not stay around the outlaws. I must not stay around Katie.* These were Jordan's waking thoughts. The one would bring dreaded consumption of the soul, the other of the heart.

He had read the Bible that Katie insisted he "borrow" until the evening light grew murky. Then he lighted a candle and read on. He read every passage of Scripture she had marked for him, then ventured into a random search. That's where he found wise Solomon's proverbs warning him against evil associates. That meant, he decided, that he must part ways with Flynn's gang, however costly the break. It would be better to die right than live wrong.

Now he pulled himself from his bunk, tired and sleepy from his late-night study. The homemade goodness of the salt-rising bread Mrs. Matterhorn sent home with him for his breakfast made him feel better.

He wanted to get to town early for two reasons. One was to avoid meeting the Matterhorns. He had promised to go to church with them on Sunday so he could return Katie's Bible, but he refused to inflict more hurt upon himself by seeing her in town again where the rescue had taken place. He would go to the village and back before the afternoon shoppers gathered.

The other reason for the morning trip was to make sure he got back to the cabin before Flynn, Pete, and Lucky came back. He had made them a promise that he would be there, and that promise must be kept.

His motive for the journey was to check the stage-coach schedules and rates. He was eager to be on his way to California. He doubted that he had enough money for a ticket, but if the outlaws got gold, they would insist on paying him for keeping the home front. It galled him to take any part of the dishonest money. However, he planned to repay his part of the stolen funds as soon as he earned it.

Even for a sore heart, it was a pleasant morning. The earth had had her bath and smelled fresh and clean, powdered with early summer scents.

As Jordan passed the only house that stood between him and the small town, a friendly young man threw up his hand. Jordan walked to the fence for a neighborly greeting.

"Luke Solomon." The man reached across the gate to shake hands. "Are you new here?"

"Yes, sir. Jordan Thomas is the name. I'm here temporarily—up at the old place in the woods. I'm on my way out west. I hope to leave on the next coach."

"Actually I don't live here." The man gave his head a jerk toward the house. He was a clean-cut man with a straightforward manner. "My mother and father—and my sister, Jennifer—live here. I have a place in town. My wife and I are staying here with Mother while Father is away. It's a pity you're not neighboring longer so we could invite you in for a meal and get better acquainted."

"I'm sure the loss is mine," Jordan responded. "But a man has to earn his bread. Where would I find the stage schedules?"

"Most any of the merchants will know the schedules. Mr. Samuelson at the saddle shop would probably have that information written down."

"Thank you." Jordan moved on.

The town was waking. Shops opened, merchants swept their floors and uncovered their wares. Some of them did all their business on this one day.

Gambler Bill put his head out the door of his infamous establishment, blinking his bloodshot eyes against the sunlight. As Jordan walked by, he stepped onto the board-walk and waved him down. "Are you the boy that lives with Flynn?"

Jordan stopped. "Yes, sir."

"Tell me, son. Will Flynn be coming in to town tonight or has he already gone to help my brothers?"

"He's gone, sir, but I don't think he had in mind helping anyone. I'm expecting him back by evening."

"When did he leave?"

"Thursday."

"Ah, that's good. A generous man, that Flynn. But a poor hand at games. When I told him that my brothers were broke down on the trail about fifty miles north of here, he offered right away to go help repair the wagons. I couldn't get away from my business to go myself."

"Your brothers were returning from the gold mines, sir?"

"Yes. Flynn said some of his own family was in the

wagon train and he wanted to get a message through to his wife—"

Jordan looked up in surprise. "I wasn't aware that Flynn had a wife."

"And a child. A little girl named Carolina. I'm surprised he never mentioned them to you."

Why had Flynn lied to the man?

"I gave Flynn directions to the camp. I'm eager for news from my brothers. Did his friend, Pete, go along, too?"

"Yes, sir."

"Ah, that Pete would make fuel for a dozen stories. . . . Well, I hope he brings word of my brothers." The man shuffled his large body back into the den.

Jordan turned his head away from the post that had caught Katie's dress as he hurried on down the street toward the saddle shop. Mr. Samuelson had not arrived, so Jordan sat on the split-log bench near the front of the store and waited.

The parson came by, introduced himself, and invited Jordan to church. Jordan promised to be there.

Mr. Samuelson, in no hurry to open his business, tied his horse to the hitching post and joined Jordan on the log seat. He was a rugged man, handsome in spite of the smallpox scars about his face. "Beautiful day."

"Yes, sir."

"You're here early."

"Can't tarry long."

"How do you like our town, son?"

"I like it, sir. The people are congenial."

"It's a quiet and peaceful town, for the most part. Our lawman, Mr. Tower, has been frustrated that he hasn't solved the two robberies that disgraced us a few weeks back, though. They struck an old gentleman and a woman. Yellow creatures, whoever they are. Me, I think the scoundrels moved on out of the country. There might not have been any connection between the two. Mr. Tower has been nettled ever since, so woe be unto the next person who makes a wrong move!"

"I came to ask about the stagecoach schedules and rates."

"You're not leaving us, are you?"

"Yes, sir. I figure a man has to find a place in life where he can make a living, and I've been informed that work is plentiful on the West Coast if a man is willing to work. I'm not afraid of hard work."

"I might be able to offer you a bit of work right here. Business is perking up. Then you wouldn't have to leave us."

"I—I have reasons for wanting to move on, sir. Personal reasons."

"Well, we'll check the lines." He unlocked his doors and Jordan followed him inside. The place smelled of leather and sawdust. "Coaches come through about every six weeks in good weather. Seems to me it's been a spell since one has been by this way." He studied a piece of paper. "Yep, looks like we're due a coach about Monday. Rates vary with distance and accommodations, of course. You'd have to work that out with the driver. They're fair and sometimes they'll take you real cheap if they're traveling light, and you are, too."

"I'll be on hand Monday. I don't want to miss that coach."

"No, because if you do, you'll have a long wait for

the next one. It's a good time of year to be cross-countrying."

Jordan went back to the cabin, took down his hidden money, and counted it. He hoped it would be enough.

Chapter 9

HOMETOWN SHOCK

"**N**ot *Matthew Solomon!*"
Greenfield, Katie's hometown,
reeled with shock. The account of
the murder of one of the city fathers reached the people
in various revised versions on Saturday.

Mr. Matterhorn heard one story at the blacksmith
shop where he went to have his plow sharpened. Lydia
listened to another in the post office. And Katie got bits
and pieces of information in Sharpe's Dry Goods Store
when she went there to buy lace for her wedding dress.

As the news circulated, business in town lagged; shops
closed and proprietors put timeworn and oft-used wreaths
on their doors. Matthew Solomon was a deacon in the
community church. He and his three married sons—Mark,
Luke and John—were loved and respected by everyone.
And his daughter, Jennifer, who played the church's
wheezy pump organ, was Katie's best friend.

Mr. Matterhorn seemed eager to get his family home.
He kept looking about nervously to make sure they were
not being followed. "I can't understand all the violence,"

he grieved. "It's unsafe *in* town or *out* of town. But of all people, why would anyone want to kill Matthew Solomon? Why, a better man never graced the earth!"

"Did you hear exactly what happened to Brother Solomon, Maynard?" Lydia asked.

"We know *what* happened, Lydia. But the hows and whys beg answers yet. The part of the story I got came straight. The parson talked to Mark, the smithy's son talked to the parson, and I talked to the smithy.

"You know John had bought some ranch land up in Montana to start running a few cattle. He planned to move his wife and the girls up there next year.

"So Matthew and Mark were going through on horseback to help John put up a cabin on the place, this being a good time of the year and all. Luke stayed here to look after all the ladyfolks.

"They were about fifty miles to the north of here when the tragedy happened. They'd stopped about noon in an out-of-the-way and sheltered place to build a fire and fetch them a bite to eat.

"Being as it had rained during the night, Mark rode off a piece to try to find some dry wood for the campfire while his father laid out the grub. He had to go farther and stay longer than he intended. When he came back, Matthew was just barely conscious. He'd been struck in the head and had a bad gash on his face. His horse was gone. He just muttered a few words to Mark before he died."

"That adds up with what I heard," Lydia said. "The postmaster said he heard say Mark saw the robbers leaving with Brother Solomon's horse, but they were too far away for Mark to tell what they looked like or how many of them there were. And of course he couldn't leave his injured father to pursue them. His father said, 'They . . . stole . . . my horse,' then he reached up and touched his face and said, 'Scars.' Perhaps he was afraid his face would be scarred if he lived. Oh, Maynard, what is going to happen next?"

Katie's lawn handkerchief caught her silent tears. "Poor, poor Jennifer and Mrs. Solomon!"

"And John's family, with John away off up in Montana," wept Lydia.

"It brings back all the memories of losing Benny," Mr. Matterhorn said. "Life will never be the same for any of them. Death has a way of turning everything brown around the edges."

"Do you think the murder will ever be solved, Maynard?"

"I think there's not a chance in a million, Lydia. There were no witnesses, Mark didn't see the gangsters, and the crime happened a day's journey from here. The posse has nothing to go on except a description of Matthew Solomon's horse."

"We can pray, Father. God wants justice to be done as badly as we do."

"Yes, Katie, we can pray. And we will."

"Could I please pass the night with Jennifer, Father? I might be of some little comfort."

"Katie has a good idea, Maynard. Jennifer needs someone her age with her during her grief. And Katie could help with the youngsters, too."

"I regret that the Solomons have no close neighbors. A body feels so desolate at a time like this. Their place is farther from neighbors than ours."

75

"The postmaster said the old Barnes place had been leased out," Lydia mentioned. "But that's on down the road a ways from the Solomons."

"The Barnes place? Why, that old house is about to tumble down!" scoffed Mr. Matterhorn. "It isn't liveable. It doesn't even have panes in the windows. When cold weather comes—"

"I don't think the renters plan to stay long."

"Father!" cried Katie. "That must be where Jordan Thomas is living. I couldn't figure out which place he was talking about. Yes, that has to be it. He said they were going on to California soon. He'll make a lovely neighbor for—" she stopped short, then ended her sentence painfully, "Jennifer."

"I thought maybe we'd see Jordan in town today. I sure took a liking to the chap. He's clean and honest like our Benny was. I intended to invite him back to visit us."

A slow flush crawled up Katie's neck and covered her ears. "I—I invited him to church tomorrow. He said he would come. May I ask him to sit with our family?"

"I'd be plumb proud if he would honor us."

"I'll fix dinner for him," Lydia offered. "It'll be like having Benny home again."

"That'll be nice, Lydia. He's away from his own folks. Life's a bumpy road when you have to travel it alone. I wonder about his background, his family . . ."

"He has no family at all, Father. But he isn't traveling alone. There are some men with him now, although he says he may go on to California from here by himself. And I meant to tell you, these men passed near our house last Monday—"

Lydia squeezed her husband's arm. "The footprints

you saw, Maynard!"

"Perhaps they were looking for a place to live that day," finished Katie.

Visible tension left Mr. Matterhorn's face. "You can't imagine how that rests my mind, just knowing it wasn't those robbers sneaking around!" he sighed. "I've been afraid to leave the place all week. But how is it you knew all this, Katie?"

Katie smiled. "I asked Jordan how he knew where we lived and he said he saw my torn dress hanging on the clothesline when he and the men came near our house."

"I wonder if he noticed the three socks."

"He did. He said he invented some sort of story of his own about them."

"A three-legged man?" laughed Mr. Matterhorn.

"He never told me what it was, but it must have been amusing. He has a golden sense of humor."

"I wonder why these men stopped over in our area? There'd certainly not be much to hold them here," Mr. Matterhorn mused.

"Jordan didn't say, Father. But I think whatever the reason, it was by God's design. Jordan's heart is searching for God. He said the strangest thing to me about the patch in my dress."

"What was that, Katie?"

"He said it was mended so beautifully, and he wished that *torn hearts* could be patched like the tear on my dress. He must have suffered a—a torn heart at some time or another."

"You witnessed to him, didn't you?"

"Yes, I told him that God was a wonderful heart

77

ailor. I let him borrow my Bible, too. He said he would return it tomorrow."

"I'm glad he decided to worship with us," her mother nodded. Then she turned toward Katie with a sudden alarm. "He does know that you are spoken for, doesn't he, Katie?"

"Yes, he knows."

"He walked to our house, but surely he has a horse, hasn't he, Katie?"

"He didn't mention one, Father." She pondered, then added. "No, I don't suppose he does. He talked about taking a coach on to California from here."

They came to a fork in the road. "Shall we just go on to the Solomon place now, Lydia?"

"No, Maynard. I have a berry pie baked at home that I'd like to take along to the Solomon family. And Katie will need to pick up a change of clothing. When did Mark get home with the body?"

"Sometime last night. They had taken a pack horse along with their supplies; Mark brought the corpse home on the pack animal."

"As cool as it is, I suppose they'll hold the body over until Monday for burial." The wagon wheel on Lydia's side jostled against a rock, causing her to grapple for support. "It's bound to be a big funeral."

At the Solomons', the long night began for Katie. She put the children to bed with bedtime stories, then she found herself telling Jennifer all about Jordan Thomas. It seemed to distract the girl's mind and keep her from dwelling on the horrors of her father's death.

"I want you to meet him, Jennifer. I think he's your closest neighbor now."

"Luke mentioned a young man passing our place this morning on the way to town, but I only half listened. Luke tries to match me up with every young man he sees. And I try to ignore his noble efforts."

"You might not want to ignore this one," Katie said. "I met Jordan quite by accident myself. He saved me from being trampled by a runaway horse in town a week ago."

"And you haven't seen him since?"

"Oh, yes! He came to my house just yesterday. In the fall I took, I lost Aunt Cynthia's photograph. Jordan found it and returned it to me. Father invited him to stay and have a meal with us."

"It was kind of him to return the locket."

"It shows his character. He's one of the nicest young men I've ever met. His eyes are kind, but there's a sadness in them, too. Like he's suffered a lot. But let me tell you how he knew where I lived—that's quite a story! He and his friends were out looking for a house to rent last Monday when he saw the dress I tore in the accident hanging on the clothesline—"

"Why were they at the back of your house?" Jennifer's eyes, red from crying, held questions. "Why didn't they come by the road to the front?"

"They were lost! Remember, they are new to our part of the country."

"And why did he wait until Friday to return your lost locket? Why didn't he knock on your door that day and give it to you then?"

Katie blushed. "I think he probably wanted to come by himself when he returned it."

"Why should you want me to meet him? It seems as though he's interested in you, not me."

79

"But I'm engaged to Ellis Shelby, Jennifer."

"So I'm to play second fiddle?" She almost smiled.

"No. When he sees you, Jennifer Solomon, he'll be smitten."

"Then I should hope to meet him—and smite him." It was an old joke between them. "How old is this Prince Charming?"

"Twentyish."

"And easy on the eyes?"

"Very!"

Jennifer pushed a delinquent black ringlet back from her forehead. "He does sound like a true gentleman, Katie. And it's been awhile since I've met one of those. They're rare."

"You can meet him at church tomorrow—" She put her hand to her mouth. "I'm sorry, Jennifer. I forgot that you won't be there. But Mother is having him to dinner. If Father will let us borrow the buggy, and if Jordan wishes, I'll bring him over to meet you."

"No harm can be done to meet him."

Darkness fell, intensified by the shadow of death that hung like a black curtain around the house. A changing wind rattled the shutters. Suddenly Jennifer bolted upright in her chair. "Katie!" She turned white.

"What's wrong, Jennifer?"

"Do all horses nicker alike?"

"I think so. Why?"

"I know that I heard Father's horse nickering outside. Maybe Charley Horse broke loose from the man who stole him and came home!"

They ran to the door, but all they heard was the retreating thunder of hooves going toward the old Barnes place.

Chapter 10

SUNWISE OR WITHERSHINS

Pete's mind reeled back over the tension-bitten hours in a fast, jerky sort of cyclorama. The day had not gone well for him.

"Flynn!" Pete had stood where his victim once lay. "Either the old man got up and walked away or someone carried him off. I know this is where he was." Fear made a bid for his emotions and won.

"There's footprints into the woods. Were they there when you got the horse yesterday?"

"I don't know, boss. I didn't take time to count footprints."

"You're a stupid bungler, Pete. All intelligent bandits know to size up the situation from every angle before they make a charge."

The criticism farther eroded Pete's confidence. He hung his head.

"And look. Horses went toward the main road from here."

"That's been since yesterday, too, boss."

"Then we'd better light out fast. Someone will be looking for a man with a scar on his face riding a black horse."

"Will they find me?"

"Not if we get this horse on home. They'd have no way of knowing where we are from or where we are going. They'd likely go west looking. That's the direction stolen horses are being taken."

"The man back at the dugout—he saw the horse, and he saw me."

"We didn't tell him anything about ourselves."

"He heard you call me Pete."

"There's hundreds of Petes."

"With scarred faces?"

"Yes. All of them. I've never met a man named Pete that didn't have a scar on his face somewhere. Sort of a trademark of the name, it seems. You're wasting time, Pete. Come on. We'd better stay off the road. We'll get on up to Colorado and you'll have no worries."

Pete pouted. "Nothing has gone right on this trip. All we got is empty pockets, deserting friends, and a dry whistle. And now we're law-dodging."

"It's because it's May. Grandpap didn't like May. Claimed it was the unluckiest of all months. It dawns on me now why Friday the thirteenth in May is scratched on so many grave markers."

"Don't say grave markers, boss."

"The date is bad news and the month is bad news. That means double trouble."

"That's what Lucky tried to tell us. We should have turned around and went home."

"Yep. We're fortunate to be alive. We should have

laid in bed under a nine-patch quilt all day."

"Sounds good to me. This grandpap of yours—he had a rich and happy life, eh?"

"He would have if it hadn't been for Grandmam. She poked fun at his notions and undid all the good luck he could have had with her skeptical attitude. She was a fanatic on religion.

"She even tried to make me think that all Grandpap's beliefs were hogwash. Laugh, she would. She'd say, 'Flynny'—I hated it when she called me that—'don't you set your heart to Grandpap's *silly superstitions.*' That's what she called them: silly superstitions. She'd cross forks and knives on the dinner plates just to nettle Grandpap. She delighted in refuting him."

"You did remember to put a horseshoe over the door of that house you rented for us, didn't you, boss?"

"The number one thing that I did was to put salt on the table. That's what you always do first when you move into a house. Then you horseshoe it. I did that second. Last I put a knife under the doormat. That's to keep witches from coming in."

"You're fortunate to know all those things."

"When I was still in nightdresses, Grandpap taught me which side of the bed to get out on. He said that was the first and most important thing of the day. Then when I was older, he taught me to put my boot on the right foot first. You always goof up if you don't do that."

"There was nothing you could do to undo your bad luck if you forgot once in a while?"

"Seems there was." Flynn drew his face into a dark study. "Let's see. What did Grandpap say?" He slapped his saddle and the black horse jumped sideways. "Yes.

It comes back to me now! If you got your boot on the wrong foot, you had to take it off and run outside. Then someone had to pitch your boot out the door to you so you could start over."

"You'd be out of luck if there was no one to pitch your boot."

"Yeah. That's why you mustn't forget."

"Shhhhh! Flynn, I hear someone coming down the road!"

"Then shut up and skeedaddle, you oaf!"

They whipped their horses into the brush, ignoring limbs that grabbed at their bodies and their clothing. Uneven terrain slowed their travel. Although the stolen horse was well-trained, Flynn's harsh commands seemed to confuse him. "This is a fine horse, Pete, but he's used to a softer man," Flynn said. "Our personalities don't match. I need a mean, stubborn horse."

"He'll do for the kid."

"If the kid's still there."

"When do we head for Colorado, boss?"

"If we're to expect a good journey, we'll have to start out when the moon is in her first quarter. In the waxing. She'll be waxing for another week yet. We'll have to go before she starts to wane. We surely don't want to have to hang around this part of the country until she waxes again next month."

"No, sir, boss! The sooner we leave, the easier I'll rest."

They rode into the evening and just after sundown drew near the Solomon place.

"Looks like a party going on here, Pete." Flynn pulled hard on the stallion's reins. "Lots of wagons around and

84

lamps ablaze. Think we could crash in and find something to drink?"

"It would be worth a try, boss. I'm thirsty enough to chance anything. We might even get invited to dance."

"I don't know how to do those new fancy dances."

"We could learn. Or fake it."

As Flynn turned toward the house, the horse threw his head and nickered. The sound was low and lonesome.

"Go, Pete!" urged Flynn, with a desperation. "This horse is acting mighty strange. I think there might be a wake going on here. Horses are smart on things like that; they can smell death. Ride, Pete, ride!"

Flynn goaded his horse into a fast gallop and raced toward the Barnes place, never looking back. Here the past and the present merged for Pete as he followed close behind, swearing at his horse's shorter legs.

Flynn tethered the animals behind the delapidated shack. Jordan met them at the back door with a candle. He held it to one side so they could see better. The wax guttered down.

"Thomas!" screeched Flynn, "hold that candle upright! If it burns one-sided, the wax will form a winding sheet and that means death!"

Jordan arighted the candle. He squinted into the semidarkness. "Where's Lucky?"

"That's what we want to know," snorted Flynn. "He shucked us. You haven't seen him around here, have you?"

"No, sir."

"Did you know when we left that he had designs on deserting us?"

"No, sir."

"Why didn't you tell us before we left, Thomas, that

yesterday was Friday the thirteenth?"

"I didn't see a calendar until . . . until after you were gone."

"We had all sorts of bad luck. First we lost your horse to a disagreeable river. Then Lucky left us during the night without a word. We didn't find any gold or any brew."

"But we did buy a beautiful stallion." Pete stood in the door. "Blacker than a washpot. We found just the one to replace your bronc, and we *bought* him!"

"What happened to the gold?" Jordan asked.

"It's in a bank in California. We didn't have time to go for it."

"And we couldn't just abandon you," Pete winked. "Could we, boss?"

"That would have been all right," Jordan said. "I'm old enough to take care of myself."

"We found a man who told us about Colorado gold," Flynn said. "There's more there than there is in California—"

"Say, Flynn!" Pete slapped him on the back. "Do you remember that rainbow the morning after the rainstorm?"

"Don't recollect that I do."

"The end of it came down toward Colorado instead of California. That rainbow was trying to tell us something. I always heard that there was a pot of gold at the end of a rainbow."

"Could be. Lucky will miss it if he took off to California. Because the California gold is already locked up in banks. We'll have the last laugh on ole Lucky. It'll serve him right for trying to get ahead of us."

"What you been doing, kiddo?" Pete was a master at switching subjects. "Any news?"

"I've been trying to clean up around here and make this place more liveable," Jordan answered. "I can't abide filth."

"Did you sweep?" asked Flynn.

"Yes, sir."

"You didn't sweep toward the door, did you?"

"What difference would it make?"

"Why, anyone knows, Thomas, that you always sweep toward the fireplace, never toward the door. Sweeping toward the door is bad luck." Flynn hastened to cross his heart to undo any damage Jordan may have done.

"When I was cleaning up," Jordan said, "I found a knife under that rotten old rug in front of the door. Seems to be a pretty good knife. I laid it there on the hearth."

"You idiot!" Flynn shouted curses at Jordan. "That knife was there to keep witches out of this house. There's no telling how many evil spirits came in when you took the obstacle away. Why, that was like letting down a gate—"

"Seems like I've messed things up pretty badly, Flynn," Jordan said, evenly, low voiced. "But I tell you what I'll do—"

"I thought you knew all about omens! You seemed to know the spell of the black and white socks on that clothesline. I can't believe you didn't know about the knife!"

"Just tomorrow I was planning on going to a place where I could learn more about how to overcome all evil. I think it would be good for me—for all of us—if I would go and learn what I can."

"Where is this place?"

"The meeting will be held in a little building over on the sunrising side of town."

"How did you find out about it?"

"A lady I met in town last Saturday told me about it. She goes to the meetings, and she never has to worry about witches or demons or spells. She has learned about a special power that can hex them all! She even gave me a black Book to study and it's really quite interesting. It gives all sorts of examples of people who were delivered from their evil influences."

"Ummm. That sounds pretty good, huh, Flynn?" Pete said. "I think he'd better go and find out about it for us."

Flynn seemed to forget his anger about the knife. "It sounds too easy, though, not to have to guard against being jinxed all the time. But it sure won't do any harm to investigate, Thomas."

"Let Jordan take the new stallion we bought and try him out, boss," suggested Pete. "That black beast ought to start him out on the *right foot*. Heh heh."

Flynn made a growling noise. His silent rebuke hung in the air like deadly fumes. No one dared move. "You're not poking fun, are you, Pete?"

"Certainly not, boss." A face had never straightened faster.

"Pete has made a good suggestion," agreed Flynn. "Thomas, you're welcome to take the new horse. Only when you take him around the house in the morning, take him around sunwise. To take him withershins would be a bad start."

"Yes, sir."

"And the clothes in the saddlebag came in the deal

with the horse. They're too Sunday-go-to-meetin' for me and Pete. You're welcome to them."

"Thank you," said Jordan. "I'll likely use them. And, if you'll excuse me, I think I'll turn in now so I will be rested up for my first lesson on the morrow."

"I think I'll bed down, too, boss." Pete spoke with lamblike meekness. "It's been a tough day."

"Is there a scrap of bread around here anywhere, Jordan?" Flynn asked.

"I picked up some bread yesterday."

"I need a little piece."

"I put it on the table to keep it from the mice. Eat as much as you'd like. It's excellent bread, baked by an excellent cook."

"I don't plan to eat it. I just wanted some to put under my pillow tonight so I will dream about our future."

Jordan blew out the candle.

"Bring us good luck, Thomas. As I recollect, tomorrow is your birthday and you'll be a man."

Chapter 11

DISCOVERY AND RECOVERY

Ellis frowned into the large beveled mirror, struggling to get his tie straight, and when he had succeeded, he surveyed his general appearance with satisfaction.

Bold, daring eyes stared back at him from the glass. A brown underlay stanchioned the bronze highlights that defied the hair oil's control. He thought himself handsome, attributing his better features to the Shelby side of the family.

"Where are you headed, Ellis?" His father passed through the hall on the way to the library with a sheaf of papers.

"To a party."

"Marriage will put a damper on your party going."

Ellis laughed merrily. "What would a party be without Ellis Quincy Shelby, married or unmarried?" With or without the amen of his own conceit, Ellis had no doubts that he was the most sought-after bachelor in the city. He liked the status.

He hoped that Katie would prove to be a party girl,

since he had no intentions of slacking his social life for
so insignificant a thing as a wife. If she didn't like parties, she could stay home—alone.

"Whose party this time?" his father asked, not bothering to slow his pace for Ellis's reply.

"Beverly Judson's."

Mr. Shelby was gone before his son's answer was com-
pleted, as if he knew what the answer would be.

Beverly. Ellis smiled. He'd gone to school with Beverly
since nursery days. Her parties never lacked pizazz (and
plenty to drink), and this evening promised to be lively.
Beverly, a buxom girl with the wiles of a snake charmer,
would have been a good candidate for marriage if she had
more money. As it was, there were too many heirs ahead
of her to claim the family fortune. It was rumored that
her eldest brother, a crooked attorney, already had his
plans laid to divert the wealth into his own pockets. Being the mayor's son gave Ellis the advantage of hearing
such things. Who wanted a girl with no substantial dowry?
Money: that was life's essence.

He called his valet. "How do I look, Culpepper?"

"Ready, Squire. Ready." The sinewy man grinned.

"Then let's go."

Beverly received Ellis at the door of her family's
estate at precisely seven o'clock, smiling her approval
while she pinned a boutonniere to his lapel. "You do look
stunning tonight, Ellis," she whispered. "I hope that I
may have the honor of a dance with you." Her perfume
was intoxicating; her expensive evening gown revealed
bare arms. These things always allured Ellis. In his mind,
he put the face of Katie into that same dress. He couldn't
get it to fit.

92

As he surveyed the gathering crowd, Ellis discovered that Beverly's gown was modest in comparison to many of the others. Katie, extracted from the portrait and put into any of these gowns, would be desecrated. Just what *would* she wear to a function such as this?

Skirts rustled, garish girls tittered, and Ellis bowed dotingly to all the ladies. This was the city's elite flaunting their wealth in finery and jewels. Where Katie would place in all this coterie, he did not know. It would be Goldie's problem to see that her niece fell nothing short of these arbiters of fashion, because this was Ellis's world, a world that Goldie said she would teach Katie to thrive in. These girls were beautiful, but mechanical and stagy. Katie would be *courtly*. He grew heady with the thought.

The revelry swung into high gear; the band Beverly hired for the occasion struck up the dance music. Ellis saw her gliding toward him and he held out his hand. "Beverly the Beautiful!" He bent in the middle and kissed her fingers. With alcohol, his personality blossomed and his tongue loosened.

They whirled about the floor, and Beverly managed to get him beyond the heavy drapes and out onto a small balcony where they could be alone.

"I saw the announcement of your bethrothal in the paper, Ellis." She puckered her ruby red lips roguishly. "Why didn't you tell me that you were getting married?"

He laughed. "I wanted to surprise you, darling."

"The New York belles are simply heartbroken, of course. When I read about it, I went directly over to Madam Goldstein's to congratulate her on the marriage of her daughter. And on the snagging of such a wonderful son-in-law." She emphasized the relationship.

"Son-in-law? Did the paper make so grave a mistake, Beverly? I can't believe it! Goldie will be quite upset."

"A mistake? You mean, Ellis, that you aren't engaged after all? Oh, Ellis, I'm—I'm so relieved!"

"The engagement isn't a mistake, but Mrs. Goldstein has no daughter. I am marrying her niece. I don't know how the society editor could have made such an unforgivable blunder."

"I see that you do not know the truth of the matter, Ellis. I was half afraid of that. And I'm ever so sorry that I am the one who brought it up." Her eyes misted, her voice suggested pity.

"I—I don't know what you're talking about."

"Of course you don't, darling." She patted his arm affectionately. "Shall I tell you or shall I forbear?"

"If it concerns me, don't keep me in the dark."

"It concerns you. But I was afraid you'd be so much in love with Katie Matterhorn that you wouldn't listen to reason."

"In love? Me? Ha!" His breath smelled of wine; his eyes shone unnaturally bright. "Love is a relative definition of a human emotion. One doesn't marry for love nowadays; one marries for advantages. Like money."

"I'm not at all sure that it would be to your advantage to marry this woman half again as old as yourself and mixed up with renegades and outlaws."

"Who are you talking about, woman?" He grappled for sobriety. "You've been misinformed."

"I'm talking about Katie Matterhorn, your lovely bride-to-be. Mrs. Goldstein has deceived you into thinking she is young, when in fact, the picture in the newspaper is at least a decade old, maybe two!"

"Where did you hear those lies?" He jerked away from her and tottered back toward the sound of the music. "If that perjury was in the newspaper, I'll sue them!"

She caught his arm. "You, dear Ellis, have been tricked." Her whispery voice stopped him. "Oh, it wasn't in the newspaper. Mrs. Goldstein saw to it that it wasn't! Katie is really Mrs. Goldstein's illegitimate child. Her father was a worthless fisherman, and the Madam adopted the child out so that no one would ever learn of her shame. Now she claims her as her niece."

"It isn't so!"

"It isn't? For your sake, Ellis, I wish it were not."

"Katie belongs to Goldie's sister."

"Can't you see what a good story that makes, Ellis?" Her tone implored him, breaking through to his befuddled mind. "She had to invent the sister so that no one would realize the child's mother was really herself. What better way to mislead people?"

"Where did you hear this trash, Beverly?"

"I got the information from an inside source—someone right inside the Madam's house. One of her personal servants, if you please! I paid a pretty penny for the investigation. Of course, it would make me no matter except that it involves you, my best friend. Many others in our social circle know about it, too. That's why you have noticed looks of sympathy tonight. It will ruin you if you marry that trollop. Such a perfect specimen of manhood wasted. And one of our own! Believe me, Ellis, no one in our class will accept her. Could you blame us? She's scum."

"Why would Goldie try to match me up with something like that? Goldie is a family friend."

"Why, indeed? It's because she is being blackmailed. The slattern daughter of hers has threatened to expose the whole ugly truth if her mother does not come up with her a wealthy New York husband. Mrs. Goldstein is afraid of her own daughter!" The music stopped and Beverly lowered her voice. "So Mrs. Goldstein is, in turn, buying you off. Be truthful, Ellis, there's money involved, isn't there?"

"Goldie has everything she owns willed to Katie, but Katie doesn't know that—"

"Katie's money won't do you a bit of good, Ellis Shelby! She'll connive to have hers and yours before it's over. And she'll spend your money building missions and charity hospitals."

"No, she won't!" Ellis' tongue moved across his lips.

"My investigation reveals that Mrs. Goldstein's daughter is antisocial. She hates parties. If you marry her . . ."

"Okay. Okay. I won't marry." He took Beverly into his arms and placed his wet lips upon hers.

"Of course you'll marry! But it won't be Miss Matterhorn that you marry. There's always others." She wrinkled her nose at him, making her paint-shaded eyes wide and appealing. "Like me, for instance."

"Yes, yes . . ."

The curtain moved to one side, and Cynthia Goldstein stood looking upon the couple locked in a tangled embrace. She cleared her throat to make her presence known.

"Ellis!" Her probing eyes held him. "You are inebriated!"

He pushed Beverly from him. "I'm sorry, Goldie. It's Miss Judson's fault."

"How did you know that Ellis was here?" demanded Beverly angrily. "You weren't invited to this party, and you aren't welcome. Go away!"

Cynthia effectively ignored her. "I need to speak with you please, Ellis. We have some very important matters to discuss tonight." She took Ellis by the arm and dragged him from the balcony, across the dance floor, and out the imposing front door while everyone stopped to stare in amused silence. Beverly followed as far as the door, fuming and mute.

When they had had their talk, Ellis was thoroughly confused.

"I will not try to defend myself against such petty gossip, Ellis," Cynthia said. "That is beneath me. And I can excuse your inappropriate behavior tonight in light of the fact that you were drunk and didn't know what you were doing. I lay that blame at the feet of that wicked Miss Judson. She would destroy your delightful future. The local girls are jealous. I expected nothing less."

"I'm sorry, Goldie."

"You owe it to yourself to make the trip to the territory and find out that the truth needs no shoring up. As my mother used to say, 'Cynthia, a lie costs more than it's worth, but the truth is worth more than it costs.' I think, Ellis that you will find that Katie is worth more than she 'costs.' She's not a minute older than her picture shows her to be. You must recognize Miss Judson's jealousy for what it is—a demon."

So Ellis made hasty preparations for his trip to claim Katie.

Chapter 12

SURPRISE ARREST

Morning pulled the red ball of sun up over the horizon. Jordan liked watching the birth of a new day. The thrill dated back to childhood when he somehow equated the fresh beginning with a better day than the one before. And although it seldom turned out that way, there was always that hope.

He considered the suit he found in the black horse's saddlebag a wonderful blessing. He had dreaded wearing his worn jeans and rawhide shirt to a church service. It had nothing to do with pride—or with Katie; it just seemed that a place so holy deserved better. He pressed the suit with a smooth, heated stone, coaxing out as many wrinkles as he could.

Flynn and Pete slept like drugged men and Jordan was glad, careful not to awaken them. He was in no mood to listen to Flynn's superstitious orders: *Be sure and don't take the horse withershins around the house. Put your right leg in your trousers first. Don't call a pig a pig. Don't pick up a knife you drop.* It was all so ridiculous. And if

Flynn awoke, he might yield to some quirk of his noxious disposition and decide not to let Jordan go to church. Or worse yet, it might dawn on his delinquent mind *where* Jordan was going.

Jordan drew up a bucket of water for the horse and scratched the animal's withers. The stallion had been well-kept and well-fed. He was gentle, seemed almost a pet. One seldom found such a good animal for sale. Pete had said they paid a dear price for him. Jordan wondered where they got the money for such a prized purchase.

He could not have told which brought him the most excitement: the prospect of a last visit with Katie before he boarded the coach to head west or hearing a Bible lesson. Katie was betrothed—his hopes were safely buried—but still her eyes lighted up when she talked to him and it made something tingle in his chest. He would return her Bible and . . .

He swung easily into the saddle. With Mrs. Matterhorn's homemade bread for a repast and transportation like this to take him to worship, who could ask for more from life? Tomorrow he would be severed from the outlaws. A rare peace suffused his whole body. He wished that it might last forever.

He rode slowly down the road, a winding trail that consisted of two narrow tracks beaten out by the coming and going of wooden wheels, hardly visible for the overgrowth. Sandwiched between the grooves were clumps of Bermuda grass that tantalized the horse. He wondered what history the scenic passage held.

As Jordan settled deeper in the saddle, enjoying his ride, something rattled in the pocket of the suit. He pulled out a scrap of paper that carried some Scripture references and the notation of a $3.27 offering received. It was dated the Sunday past.

It made Jordan feel good that the man who sold the horse and the suit to Flynn and Pete must have been religious. The name, *Matthew Solomon,* was written across the bottom of the note. He sat a little taller; he could wear the clothes proudly knowing that a Christian had owned them. It seemed somewhat ironic that the man's suit, obviously worn to church just a week ago, was going back to church on the back of a different man. And the man who wore it today, although not yet a Christian, wished to be one.

It almost seemed that the long-necked stallion knew the area, knew where he was going. A house, where he had stopped to chat with the young man yesterday, came into view. The horse slowed as if he thought this was Jordan's destination.

As Jordan passed, he saw a girl about Katie's age standing on the porch. The man had mentioned a sister. A pretty girl she was, and in her hand she held a bouquet of wildflowers. He tipped his hat in a gentlemanly greeting. Then his horse neighed, and the girl covered her face with her hands and fled into the house in fright.

Jordan considered reining up to see what the girl's problem might be but reasoned that if the sight of the big horse scared her, he would only intensify her fears by going closer. Some girls were frightened of horses. So he kicked the big horse into a fast gallop to be out of her sight as soon as possible and trouble her no more. When he glanced back, the young man was staring down the road after him.

His route to church took him directly through the

101

CASEY TOWNSHIP LIBRARY
CASEY, ILLINOIS 62420

center of Greenfield. The town was sure to be deserted on a Sunday with all the businesses closed. Today's memories were less painful. Some of yesterday's anguish had passed. He was thankful for that, and he even slowed when he passed the place where he had rescued Katie from the runaway horse. The post she had snagged her dress on, the place where he had found the locket—these were all strokes that helped paint the picture of the day he would remember forever. Would she always remember him? Even when she lived in her cocoon of luxury?

Absorbed in these thoughts, Jordan did not see the racing horse until the rider was upon him.

"Halt!"

"Whoa, boy." Jordan pulled the stallion to a standstill, surprised to find the barrel of a gun pointed toward his rib cage. Was this a holdup? He had no money on him.

The constable tapped his badge with a big finger. It made a clicking noise. His face was grim. "Officer Tower. Dismount and put your hands in the air."

Jordan obeyed, puzzled.

"You are under arrest."

"What for, sir?"

"Don't play innocent, young man. Every sheriff in the territory is looking for you."

"For me?"

"Hand me that Bible, and let's have your hands in these cuffs."

Jordan offered no resistance.

"Where had you started?"

"To church."

The constable sneered. "First time I've ever heard that alibi from a murderer."

"You must be mistaken, sir. I'm no murderer."

"What more evidence does a lawman need? You're riding the dead man's horse. You have the unmitigated gall to wear the dead man's clothes. And—and I'm not believing my eyes—you even have his *Bible!*" He held up the Book. Then he reached into Jordan's pockets and emptied them. "And what have we here? Ummm. More evidence. Matthew Solomon's record of last Sunday's church offering. The dead man's name is in your pocket! A careless criminal, aren't you?"

"The Bible belongs to a young lady—"

"You are caught redhanded. All of your lies won't help a thing. I can't figure why anyone would want to kill a good man like Deacon Solomon."

"I didn't kill anyone."

"What's your name?"

"Thomas, sir. Jordan's the first name."

"I mean your *real* name."

"Jordan Thomas, sir."

"Where are you from, Thomasor?"

"Hoffman."

"How old are you?"

"Twenty. No, I'm twenty-one."

"Make up your mind."

"I just turned twenty-one today."

"You're mighty young to commit such a heinous crime—a crime that must have been preplanned and premeditated. What was your motive?"

"I don't know what you're talking about, sir."

"How do you account for the horse?"

"The horse doesn't belong to me."

"That's what I've been trying to tell you, young man.

That's the first truth you've spoken. It belonged to the late Mr. Solomon."

"I know nothing of the previous owner, sir. A couple of friends of mine—or I should say acquaintances—bought this horse two or three days ago somewhere north of here. They brought him in late last evening. They gave me permission to ride him to church today."

"Your story is one of the best inventions I've ever heard, Thomasor, but not good enough to convince me to turn you free. I'd have this whole town on my back if I did that. Where could I find these two supposed friends of yours?"

"We've been camped about three miles west of town, sir. We all live together in an old rundown place out there. I forget what they call the place. The road is almost grown over with weeds."

"The old Barnes place?"

"Yes, I believe that's the name of it."

"I need the names of those friends you mentioned."

"Flynn and Pete."

"Last names?"

"I don't know, sir. I haven't been with them very long."

"Where are they from?"

"I'm afraid I couldn't answer that, either. I can only say where they were headed—to California for work."

"You're a slippery one."

"Can you tell me why I am being apprehended, sir?"

"The game goes two ways. You're stingy with your information. I can be stingy with mine. The judge will make you talk—or if you'd rather not, you can take your secrets with you to the gallows."

"I have no secrets."

"Mr. Thomasor, I believe in giving the devil himself a fair trial. And I know that if I put you in my jail in this town, a lynching mob will hang you before you can make your confession properly. Our judge is gone down to the capital for two weeks. I can't sit and guard you twenty-four hours a day to keep you from your premature death, so I'll be bound to take you to another town and let you sit in prison there until the honorable judge gets back from his meeting. In the meantime, I'll be checking on the friends you mentioned and see what they have to say for themselves. Maybe they'll be more willing to talk than you are. If your story checks out, I'll make proper apologies to you. You understand that this is my job."

"Yes, sir."

"There's been some things going on in our town that we won't tolerate and I'm thinking there may be a connection here. There's been a few robberies, one old man tied up . . ."

"Take me wherever you wish, sir."

"I'll collect the horse, the clothes, and the Bible for evidence, of course."

"Yes, sir."

They rode for half a day.

"Murderer," Mr. Tower said when he turned Jordan over to the jailer in Stafford. "Maximum security."

"I've never let a prisoner escape my hands yet." The giant of a man with brushy brows and a haystack of straw-colored hair studied Jordan with piercing eyes. Jordan made direct eye contact with his appointed guard, yet did not flinch.

"I've heard of your fame and the repute of the Stafford jail," Mr. Tower continued. "That's the reason I brought him here. Greenfield has never had a more cold-blooded crime nor a bolder criminal. I don't want word out where he is, or he'll never live to trial."

"Yes, sir." The jailer saluted, clamped a massive hand on Jordan's arm, and locked him up.

Jordan did not sleep at all that night. *Murder.* The one awful word raked across his mind again and again. He was in serious trouble—trouble that was not of his making. And he would very likely die for a deed he did not commit. *Why did I ever get tangled up with dishonest men?* he asked himself, unable to answer his own question.

A verse he read in Katie's Bible came to him now: "Lo, I am with you alway, even to the end . . ." *The end.* He knew that, barring a miracle, the end was near for him.

In the black, predawn hours of searching, Jordan hemmed up the raveled edges of the case. Flynn and Pete had robbed and killed a man and then took his horse. They would pin the awful crime on him to save their own necks. Or they would skip the country and leave the evidence to mock him. If they heard of the arrest—which they surely would—and left town, Mr. Tower would be justified in believing that Jordan had lied when he checked out Jordan's story and found the old house abandoned.

Flynn's words came back to torment Jordan: "None of us plan to get caught—ever. But we sometimes get the rap for something we don't plan on or didn't do." So that's why Flynn took him on. As a scapegoat. The job in California was just an empty promise all the time.

A fragile thread of hope looped around Jordan's heart. *If Lucky could be found, he'd defend me,* thought Jordan. He recalled the strange look in Lucky's eyes the last time he saw him—as if he were trying to get a message across to Jordan. But even as the winged thought was born, it died. Jordan would be sentenced and hanged before Lucky could be located. Sentence for a crime so violent as murder would not be delayed to comb the nation for a possible witness. The horse. The clothes. The note in the pocket of the suit with the man's name on it. They were all evidence against him. And if Flynn and Pete stayed around, there would be at least two false witnesses that would agree at the trial.

Would he ever see Katie again? Likely not. Would she get her Bible back? He hoped so. When Katie heard the news of the murder, she would surely know that he was innocent—that he would never commit such a crime.

Or would she?

Chapter 13

MAN MISSING

Katie wished that she had eyes in the back
of her head. Each time the door scraped
open, she tethered an urge to turn
around and see if it was Jordan Thomas who entered the
church. She reached up to push the three pearl combs
deeper into the upsweep of burnished curls, for Jordan's
benefit.

Mr. Matterhorn left a space at the end of the splintery
pew, traditionally occupied by the Matterhorn family, for
the visitor. But Jordan did not come.

A disappointment, in much greater proportion than
Katie expected, left her feeling weak and empty. The
parson's lesson was wasted on her unhearing ears. Her
mind strayed outside the building, began its search for
Jordan. Where was he? Why had he not come? She had
been so sure that he was a true man, genuinely interested
in righteousness.

At dismissal, the loss of their church elder blotted up
the attention of the congregation; their conversation yield-
ed nothing else. If Katie's inattentiveness was noticed,

it would be laid to her sitting the night with Jennifer and a lack of sleep. When everyone shook hands with everyone else, Katie extended her hand and pasted on a smile.

"Jordan is missing himself a good dinner," commented Mr. Matterhorn when they started for home. "I thought surely he'd be to church today."

"He said that he would come," Katie said. "Something must have happened." To her own ears, her voice echoed from the hollow of her heart.

"You don't suppose his company moved on?" Lydia asked. "He said they were headed for California."

"He wouldn't have left without returning my Bible."

"He may have posted it," suggested Lydia.

"Or he may have been called out of town temporarily," Mr. Matterhorn said. "That would seem likely since he wasn't in town yesterday, either. I don't think he deliberately missed church after giving his word he'd be there."

"I cooked extra," Lydia said, "thinking Jordan would be our guest. It's too much for our family. I shouldn't like the food wasted. Do you think we could take it over to the Solomons' and share it with them, Maynard?"

"That would be nice, Lydia, but Katie is tired—"

"I'm all right, Father. Really. Jennifer and I did get a little sleep last night. I think I would rather be there than—than sitting home alone today. Don't worry about me, please."

When the Matterhorns arrived at the slain deacon's home, Mrs. Solomon met them at the door with a distressed look. "I'm so glad you've come! Please do come in. Jennifer is in bed with a sick headache; she had quite a jolt this morning. In fact, we are all much disturbed by what has happened."

"Has something *else* happened, Mrs. Solomon?" Lydia took her hand.

"Let me tell you about it. Jennifer went out this morning to pick some wild honeysuckle and nosegays to make a funeral wreath for her father. She'd gathered the flowers and got as far back as the front porch when the whinny of a horse attracted her attention. She looked up to see a man riding on Matthew's horse, Charley. And the man was dressed in Matthew's clothes!" Mrs. Solomon's mouth twitched. "It shocked Jennifer so badly that she stumbled into the house and went into a faint."

"It was a vision, of course," Lydia said. "Poor darling. The stress is too much for her."

"No, it was real. Mark rushed out to see what had frightened Jennifer. He saw the horse and rider racing away—and it was, indeed, Charley Horse, though the man was too far away for Mark to have a good look at him."

"Why, Mrs. Solomon! How cruel of the murderer—"

"We can't figure it. Why would the man who committed such an atrocity want to come back here to taunt us? The crime happened fifty miles away. It seems the slayer would want to stay as far away from Greenfield as he could to keep himself from being apprehended. He must be demented!"

"Then the murderer knew Matthew? Knew where you lived?"

"We have no way of knowing. It's all such a mystery. I'm so sorry for Jennifer. She is just distraught!"

"Of course she is." Lydia turned to Katie. "Katie, why don't you see if you can console her. Get her mind on something else."

When Katie slipped into Jennifer's room, the girl broke into a fit of sobbing. "Oh, Katie!" She moved the damp cloth from her forehead. "Now I know that it was Charley Horse that I heard neighing last night! The man who killed my father is here somewhere. And—he may kill the rest of us, too!"

"There. There. Jennifer, we'll pray. God has promised to protect us."

"Then why didn't He protect my father, Katie? He was a deacon in the church and the most honest man that ever lived."

"I don't know." Katie squeezed her friend's hand. "Some things we must not try to understand with human reasoning. God looks from the top side, while we look up from the bottom. He sees things differently. But He said He'd give His angels charge over us. We can be sure He doesn't want us to live in fear. Here, let me help you with the wreath." Katie gathered the wilting flowers and greenery.

Jennifer made an effort to compose herself. "How was church?"

"Difficult."

"The young man—was he there?"

"No. But he'll probably show up next Sunday. Father suggested that he probably got called out of town. It'll be better for him to come when you're there, anyhow." Katie wove the wild blooms into a circle as she talked. "The singing is pretty dead without you to play the hymns for us. It's hard to stay on key without music."

"That's what Father always said."

"I wish I could play."

"Soon you will, Katie. When you are married to Ellis,

you'll have a grand piano. But oh, I don't like to think about your leaving! Now with Father gone, church will seem so—so *lonely.*"

A part of Katie rebelled against being reminded of Ellis. Of late she had invested her thoughts in Jordan, not her husband to be. The dreams of Ellis that once ignited her heart now left her cold. *Why?* She put the problem away, determined to take the wrappings off soon and examine it more closely.

After dinner, while Lydia gathered up her dishes, Mr. Matterhorn asked if Katie and Jennifer would like to ride along with him to the Barnes place to see if Jordan might be there. "It's not very far on down the road," he said. "It would be a shame to come so close and not check to make sure our friend is well—if that's where he lives."

Jennifer excused herself because of the headache but insisted that Katie go with her father. "If you find any lilacs along the way, please pick them, Katie," she requested. "They were Father's favorite flowers."

The road on from the Solomon property was little more than brushy ruts, and they were almost upon the old building before they saw it. "I thought it was right here," Mr. Matterhorn looked around, perplexed.

"There's an old shack of some sort behind those trees," pointed Katie. "See. There's a doorway."

"Yes, that's the place."

An unshaved face appeared in the opening, then vanished.

"Surely Jordan doesn't live here, Father."

"I should hope not." Mr. Matterhorn climbed from the wagon and went to inquire. A short, grizzled man answered the knock, and when he stepped into the sunlight, Katie saw that one cheek bore an ugly scar from his eye to his chin. They had come to the wrong place. This man was not Jordan's kind. Jennifer must not learn that such a character lived nearby; she would be more frightened than ever.

Katie closed her eyes against a disturbing thought that this man could be Deacon Solomon's murderer—as if by shutting her eyes she could keep out the unsolicited intuition. She shuddered.

The conversation, carried on the clear air, reached Katie with adequate volume. "I'm looking for a Jordan Thomas, sir." Mr. Matterhorn kept an anxious eye toward the buggy. "Would you know where he lives?"

"He lives right here. But he's gone today. He left early this morning and hasn't returned. Why do you want him?"

"Who is it, Pete?" roared a voice from inside the house.

"Don't know, Flynn. Someone asking áfter the kid."

"I'm Maynard Matterhorn, a friend of Jordan's, and I—"

"Tell him Thomas went to a séance somewhere," the background voice yelled.

"Went where?" Mr. Matterhorn asked.

"It's a place to learn how to turn bad luck into good luck. It's over on the sunrising side of town where they're giving the lessons. He did some things yesterday to bring us bad luck. Like he took the knife from under the mat while we were gone. And he swept toward the door. So to make up for it, he went to learn how to undo the damage he did. But it wouldn't surprise me if the spirits got angry and did him in. You don't fool with that hocus-

114

pocus stuff." He drew an imaginary cross on the front of his shirt.

"Jordan promised to join us at church this morning."

"Jordan—at *church?* Thomas? That has to be a joke, mister." He let out a raucus howl. "Never! You wouldn't catch a one of our gang in church. That's the last place Thomas would go."

"He had my daughter's Bible—"

"Nope. you got the wrong Jordan Thomas by the shirttail."

"What's the man's business here, Pete? Tell him to be gone." The command thundered from inside. Katie felt her whole body shaking.

"Pipe down, Flynn. He ain't going to barge in and stoke your fire." He turned to Mr. Matterhorn with a satanic smile. "Don't pay no mind to Flynn. He's had too much grog today."

"Just tell Mr. Thomas that Mr. Matterhorn and his daughter came by."

"What kind of horn came by?"

"*Matter*horn."

"Well now, if it don't matter, why did you mention it?"

"He would probably remember me if you just gave him my first name: Maynard."

"Maynard. May-May-May. May-nard. No, sir. I couldn't speak that. May is unlucky."

"Then you might say that I'm the man who had a daughter that he saved from a runaway horse in town."

"*Daughter?*" Pete leered, took an eager step forward. He squinted toward the wagon, but Mr. Matterhorn hastened to get Katie away from the drinking men.

"Father!" Katie clutched her father's arm. "Do you think Jordan really lives there?"

"Apparently he does. And if so, he's not the man we took him to be." He shook his head. "It pains me to think I could be so easily deceived by a man."

"But his eyes were true!"

"Yes, but the Bible says two can't walk together except they be in agreement. And there's an old worn-out saying, 'Birds of a feather flock together.' I want to believe in Jordan, but he's in a bad flock."

"Where did the man say Jordan had gone?"

"It sounds as though he's mixed up with some sort of witchcraft."

"No, Father." Katie's chin went up in a gesture of fierce defense. "No matter what the man said, Jordan has a deep thirst for God. And he'll settle for nothing less than a personal experience with his Maker."

"I hope you're right, Katie." He let the reins fall slack. "But sometimes a woman is fooled by a man who is seeking her hand instead of God's."

Chapter 14

THE CONSTABLE'S VISIT

"Looks like rain, boss."

Flynn nodded. "Yep." He reached for the scrap of lye soap lying on the weathered board that served as a washstand, unpainted and gray with age. His face and arms caught most of the water that he splashed up from the granite foot tub. "It's been puckering up for two days. That's why I delayed our moving on. I knew wet was coming, and I didn't want to be caught out in it."

"How did you know?"

"The horns of the new moon turned uppermost. An upturned moon holds water like a gourd cup, and the water is bound to spill over onto the earth after a while. Remember Saturday night when we rode in with the horse? The new moon was holding the old moon in her arms; you could see just a trace of the full moon between her horns. That always means rain."

"I passed by the cemetery and saw a family trying to get a body into the ground quick-like ahead of the weather. Must have been some maw who had an awful

big litter. There was a heap of mourners on hand to do
the wailing."

"A burial on Monday? I hope they didn't leave the
body over Sunday."

"Is that bad?"

"It's bad. Means another death in the family."

"But we're not to talk about the deep-six, boss. I don't
like to think about it. Gives me the willies." Pete moved
close to Flynn and dipped his hands into the tub, too.
"Don't you think Jordan stole our pretty black horse and
left to join himself with Lucky?"

Flynn knocked Pete away. "Pete! You should know
better than that!"

"Than what, boss?"

"Better than to wash your hands in the same dish at
the same time I'm washing. That's one of the unluckiest
things a friend can do."

"I've never heard that. Boss, you gotta give me time
to catch on. I'm just in learning school, my mind's slow,
and I didn't have a grandpap like yours. What evil did
I bring on us this time?"

"When two wash their hands in the same bowl,
they're bound to quarrel before long."

"Is there any cure for the cuss?"

"We can try. You'll have to empty the tub and start
over with fresh water. Then we'll wash one at a time. And
when we dry, we'll wring the towel between us."

"Sure, boss." Pete picked up the chipped and battered
container and sloshed the water out the window.

"No, Pete! You *never* put water out a *window.*"

Pete looked sorry. "Aw, boss, I bad-lucked us again,
didn't I?" He went to the well for more water and re-

turned with his head lowered. "But yesterday was a good day, boss," he reminded, making a feeble effort to humor Flynn. "We found money."

The word worked like magic to divert Flynn's ill-will. "Any day is good when we find money. I was afraid we'd have to take up another collection before we started on our journey. Did you know, Pete, that if you spit on the first money you take in on any particular day, the money buys more?"

"You spit, didn't you?"

"I spat."

"I guess Thomas thought we'd never find his stash. I don't believe he ever spent a penny of what you gave him. I guess we shouldn't have pilfered his part that once."

"I don't feel any remorse. He's not worth what he's getting. He's got jelly for a spine. Won't put himself out to help us steal. He don't even make a good doorstop. I had a mind to shoot him when he went back and tried to untie the old man we tied up. Think of it on this wise, Pete: this money doesn't near pay for our black horse that he took yesterday."

"You're right, boss. But he hid his money pretty good, didn't he?"

"I'd never have found it if I hadn't lifted the old crock to see where that black widow spider went."

"Beats me why he didn't take his money along with him if he didn't plan on coming back."

"I'll wager he got off in such a rush, he forgot all about it."

"If he ever returns, it'll be gone."

"And so will we."

"But I got a feeling Jordan don't plan on ever being back to collect his savings."

"Did you see his black look when we mentioned Colorado? He had his head set on California."

"Yep. He's headed that way today, or my name's not Plundering Pete."

Thunder rolled across the sky, banging from cloud to cloud. "Hear that thunder?" Flynn looked up. "The milk will sour, sure as thunder. Thunder always sours milk."

"This old place hasn't got windowpanes, boss. How are we going to keep the water out?"

"We won't be here long enough to fret about water. But if this place had windows, I'd have smashed them out."

"Why for?"

"Because if either of us saw the new moon through glass, she'd be upset with us for her whole cycle. Twenty-eight days. And on our trip, we don't need an angry moon. Always look at a new moon straight on, Pete."

"I will, boss. Soon as the rain lets up, we'll head on for Colorado, won't we?"

"We will for sure. I see no call to stay here longer. I'm ready to shuck this place like a dirty shirt."

"My fingers are itching for that gold." Pete scratched his nose. "My nose is itching, too. Don't that mean something?"

"On which side is it itching?"

"Right side."

"Company's coming. A man."

An urgent knock shook the termite-weakened walls. Pete grinned. "There he is now, boss."

120

"Better answer it quick, Pete. Whoever it is might come on in unannounced, thinking nobody's here, if you don't." Flynn scrambled for his gun. "If it's the same man as yesterday, have him bring his daughter in for us to get a better look at."

Pete stumbled to the door. "Law officer, boss," he called back. "Wants to talk to us about Thomas."

"Bring him on in, Pete."

Mr. Tower looked from Pete to Flynn. "Are either of you sober enough to answer a few questions?"

"Had nary a drop to drink," Flynn vowed. "Neither of us. Ask on."

"Mr. Thomasor said that he lived here. Is that correct?"

Flynn nodded, silencing any answers Pete might offer with one warning glance. Pete knew the eye signal well. "Yes, sir."

"I arrested Mr. Thomasor in town a few hours ago," the lawman said. "He told me that he had a couple of friends here who knew about the black horse on which he was riding. He said it belonged to you, that you had bought it—"

"No, sir." Flynn showed no emotion. "The boy lied to you. The black horse with one white stocking belonged to the boy. It never was ours."

"Where did he get the horse?"

"I'm not given to tattling."

"You'd best come up with something substantial to defend yourself, sir. The young man said that you bought and owned the horse. That particular horse was stolen and his owner murdered in cold blood. Someone will hang for the crime."

121

"I guess we'd better tell the sheriff the whole story, Pete."

"Yeah. You go ahead, Flynn. Your English is better than mine." Pete gave his head an affirmative tilt for Mr. Tower's benefit.

"We were right sure that the boy committed a crime, sir. It happened about fifty miles to the north of here. We had taken him with us to see some relatives of Gambler Bill's. If you need to prove my story about the visit, you can talk to old man Bill himself. He gave me the directions to find his brothers. They were camped thereabouts, going back to Miz Carolina. I wanted them to take a message through to my wife and little girl who live where they were going.

"Well, sir, on the way there, Thomas's horse got caught in a whirlpool and swept downriver . . ."

"The man's name is Thomas?"

"Yes, it's Thomas, sir."

"First initial?"

"J."

"*J. Thomasor.*" The officer wrote the name on his tablet. "Go on with your story."

"After he lost his horse, he couldn't go on with us—or get back home either—without another one. So he left us around noon—that was on Friday the thirteenth—while we were cooking up a meal. Said he was going to buy him a horse and would be back to continue on the trip with us.

"We waited a considerable time, and by and by, he came back with the horse. He told us he bought it from a middle-aged gentleman but had to give an unreasonable price for it. We noticed there was blood on his clothes. It made us suspicious, since he had no money that we

122

knew of to buy a horse like that.

"He took off the old clothes and put on a Sunday-go-to-meeting garb that he found in the saddlebag. He said he was pleased that the man sold him the clothes, too. Then he dropped his old blood-splattered clothes in the first river we came to. It made us almighty nervous, didn't it, Pete?"

The mute man tipped his head again. "Ummmm."

"But of course, we had no proof of foul play so we didn't let on—"

"Exactly where were you camped?"

Flynn gave the location of the murder.

"It matches up. What Mr. Thomasor didn't take into consideration is that the victim's son was in the woods nearby gathering firewood. He came back before his father died."

"He did? Was—was he able to give a description of the man who took his horse?" Pete rubbed the scar on his face.

"No. He only said a few words before he passed on."

"That's too bad." Pete took his hand from the scar.

"Then Mr. Thomasor made another bad move. He came back to the victim's hometown. Mr. Solomon, who had started to Montana to help an older son build a house, was a deacon in our community church."

"You mean the man who owned the horse lived here?"

"He was your closest neighbor. They had his funeral yesterday—"

"That must have been the burying you saw yesterday, Pete."

"Mr. Solomon was well thought of. Most of the town turned out for the graveside farewell. I was there myself.

123

Mr. Solomon was a dear friend of mine."

"Where is Thomas, sir?"

"He is in jail awaiting trial. I refuse to tell anyone where he is—even you. If word should get out, there would be no trial. He'd be hanged by an angry mob before sundown. I believe in justice and am determined that Mr. Thomasor has a fair trial however brutal his crime. A lot of people don't hold with my views. But I've seen men that had every evidence against them proved innocent at the last minute. We, as lawmen, can't be too careful when it comes to handing out a death sentence. I'm a Golden Rule man, and as long as I am elected to this position, I'll have it my way."

"When will this trial be?"

"Our judge is out of town, and we'll be obliged to await his return. I'm not for dragging things out, but I'm not for rushing them, either. Justice has a strange way of finding her own path, and I don't try to block her way. When the judge gets back—and not until—I'll have the criminal brought here for sentencing."

"We are headed for Colorado. We have a job waiting for us there, and we'll be leaving tomorrow—" Flynn began.

"Mr. Thomasor said you had started to California."

"Another of his tall tales." Flynn turned to Pete. "Wonder why he would tell the sheriff something like that, Pete?"

"One lie is as good as another," Mr. Tower said. "The reason I came is to inform you that both of you will have to testify at the hearing. You can't leave town until after the trial. You are hereby being subpoenaed, and if you disappear before the trial, you will be found and prosecuted. I'm sure you will not mind being a witness in this case. You are aware that you will be our key witnesses."

"We won't mind at all, sir." Flynn's eyes didn't move.

"Thank you, gentlemen. Now if I don't hurry back to town, I'll get myself wet." He sprinted to his ground-tied horse.

"Well, what do you make of that, Flynn?" Pete asked when Mr. Tower was gone. "You handled it just perfect."

"I think, Pete, if you hadn't changed out that wash water, things wouldn't have turned out in our favor."

"Did you hear what he said, boss? The man we stole the horse from lived right here in this town!"

"That's Friday the thirteenth luck. Now we know why the horse acted like he did when we went by the house where he was used to turning in."

"So when Thomas started to that séance, someone recognized the horse and turned him in to the law."

"He was caught on his birthday."

"And just think, boss, if we hadn't come in at night, we'd have been found with that horse, and it would have been us stuck with the death sentence."

"I had a feeling when we took on Jordan that we'd need him for something like this. It was a *sensation,* and I've learned to listen to these hunches. Now Pete, we're going to have to walk soft until after the trial. No more collections."

"Leastwise we have Thomas's money He won't be coming back to claim it."

"No, and come Saturday, I'll go to town and double it for us. Old Gambling Bill won't know what rapped him—he won't know that I spat on that money to make it lucky. Anyhow, I need to tell him all about Thomas stealing that horse just in case he's called on to witness or to jury. We need as many on our side as we can get. I don't hanker for a rope around my neck."

"Just to celebrate us not getting the outside of our necks hurt, boss, I sure could use a good strong drink going down inside my neck with a little of Thomas's money. How about it?"

"You couldn't get a quarrel out of me about that!"

Chapter 15

THE BLACK BOOK MYSTERY

"**A** letter for you, Katie."

Supposing that the letter was from Ellis Shélby, Katie took it from her father and went to her room. Ellis's letters no longer brought her a girlish thrill. She had no heart to read another monotonous epistle about the wealth they would have. Money! What was money? It couldn't bring happiness. The closer the time came for his arrival, the more she shrank from any reminder of marriage to the unseen suitor.

A nagging erosion ate away at her peace of mind. It was time for an open confrontation with herself. She must face her errant heart and disarm the hidden enemy.

Before she opened the letter—before she brought herself to task—she knelt beside her bed to pray. She distrusted her own reasoning; she needed a wiser, broader overview. As she communed with God, her prayers became intense, intercessory. Presently, she realized it was not for herself that she struggled, or even for Ellis. It was for Jordan Thomas. A heaviness buckled itself around her soul, and she could not unclasp its grip.

The letter lay on the bed, forgotten. More than an hour later, she picked it up, chiding herself for the distaste she felt at having to read a letter from Ellis at all. But when she opened it, she found that the handwriting did not belong to Ellis. His penmanship sent hard letters marching across the page like soldiers that never broke rank. This script, on paper that smelled of lavender, was loose and round with free characters that seemed to romp and play.

Katie read two or three confusing paragraphs, then decided the letter had been missent. She could identify with none of the text. It had begun, "Dear Katie Matterhorn," but there must be another Katie Matterhorn somewhere.

She read on into the third paragraph, no less perplexing. "We know of your deplorable background," it said. "You cannot hide your past. You are concealing nothing. . . ."

It rather amused Katie that such a letter should be misdirected to her, a girl who had been reared by godly, sin-hating parents. The one for whom the letter was intended had taken root in a different atmosphere.

"You must have some nervous skeletons in your closet," the letter continued, "but skeletons have a way of rattling out of their dark corners. And that's what yours have done."

On went the accusations: "We know that you, Katie Matterhorn, are living a lie."

There! Now she knew that she had someone else's mail.

"You are really the daughter of Cynthia Goldstein . . ."

Wait. This was ludicrous. Cynthia Goldstein, her aunt, had no daughter. What a mixup!

". . . and that you have bribed your mother into purchasing Ellis Shelby for your husband."

Katie frowned. How could it be that the author of this sordid material knew both her aunt and Ellis?

"When you come to New York as Mrs. Ellis Shelby, we do not plan to accept you. We will make life so miserable for you, you will wish you had never married into our social circle. We will expose you and your deceitful life."

The letter rambled on, seesawing from threats to defamation until Katie didn't know whether to laugh or cry, to be angry or have pity on the writer. Its outrage left her stunned, numb.

It was signed "Beverly Judson." There was no return address.

Katie sat staring at the wall; the letter slid to the floor. One thing became clear: she would be moving into a hostile sphere when she married Ellis, a world that did not want her there.

Her partly finished wedding dress lay across a chair. All morning her fingers had worked along the yards of lace while her mind slipped across the miles in search of Jordan Thomas. Now she would like nothing better than to put the dress out of her sight and forget it. She had no more desire to go to New York than her unknown foe had to have her there.

She laid her head on her folded arms and thought. Should she trouble her mother with the details of the disgraceful letter? No. It would only make her mother, who had such high hopes for her future, feel bad. Her mother did not understand the fierce battle that raged within her at this moment. This was her own battle; one she must wage—and win—alone.

She felt, though, that she must bare her heart to someone or its weight would sink her to despair. So she picked up the awful letter, dropped it into her pocket, sought out her father, and asked if he would take her to see Jennifer Solomon.

Jennifer had gone to the cemetery to place fresh flowers on her father's grave. "Leave Katie to visit with us a spell," Mrs. Solomon insisted of Mr. Matterhorn. "Jennifer will be home presently. She needs Katie's company. Mark will bring Katie home."

When Jennifer returned, she took Katie to her room where they could be alone. "Something is bothering you, Katie," she said. "I can see it in your eyes. Can I help?"

"Am I so transparent, Jennifer?"

"You are."

"You have enough hurts of your own without mine, too."

"To help someone else eases one's own pain."

"It—concerns my wedding." Katie pulled the letter from her pocket. "I received this message today from enemies I didn't even know I had." She handed the envelope to Jennifer. "See what you make of it. It sounds as though I am headed into unfriendly territory."

Jennifer read the letter and gave Katie a twisted smile. "It's blackmail, Katie. It sounds like pure jealousy to me. That girl, whoever she is, wants the man you are getting. A lot of smut goes on when there's money involved. The letter isn't worthy of your attention. Burn it—and forget it."

"I—I almost wish the girl would take Ellis off my hands."

"Katie!"

"I mean it, Jennifer. I'm having second thoughts about marrying someone I have never even seen. Now if I knew he'd be like Jordan . . ."

"Well, he won't be. And you should not expect him to be. No two men are alike. Jordan has his good points, and Ellis will have his. He might be even nicer than Jordan."

"I'm afraid that wouldn't be possible."

"Katie Matterhorn, I believe you are in love with this Jordan fellow when you are supposed to be in love with Ellis Shelby."

"I just might be." She bit at her lip. "Jennifer, is one bound to marry a person they've never met when the wedding is arranged by others?"

"I don't know the laws, Katie. Did you give your word that you would marry Ellis? Did you make a promise?"

"Yes. And he has it in writing. But I think I'd like to change my mind."

"It's probably too late now. Ellis is already on his way here, isn't he?"

"I'm afraid so."

"And think of how disappointed your Aunt Cynthia will be if you back out now. And your mother. And your father."

"Father wouldn't be disappointed."

"I can't understand you, Katie. Any girl in the world would give her shoe spoon for the chance you're getting. A grand estate—with how many rooms?"

"Fifteen."

"A cook, a maid, a butler, a gardener, a grand piano. What more could anyone want?"

Katie's hand busied itself picking at her skirt. She was silent for a long time. "I know I should be happy, Jennifer. But it isn't here." She put her hand on her bosom.

"I would be dancing up and down if I were in your place."

"I was until—"

"Until what?"

"Until the Saturday in town when Jordan rescued me from the runaway horse and I looked into his eyes."

"You sound like a silly little girl with a crush!"

"I—can't seem to help myself. I pray for him every day even though I don't know if I shall ever see him again."

"It's infatuation, Katie. You loved Ellis until this stranger came along."

"I'm not sure I ever loved Ellis. I think perhaps I was in love with the *idea* of love. But now my heart tells me that I would rather live in a log cabin with Jordan than in a mansion with Ellis."

"Well, since Jordan is gone, you can forget him and get on with your life."

"He'll be back, but I may not be here when he returns."

"What makes you so sure he'll be back?"

"He has my Bible and I know that he will see that it's returned to me."

"Your Bible!" Jennifer jumped up. "I'm glad you mentioned it. Somehow your Bible got mixed in with some things Mr. Tower returned to us this morning—things that belonged to my father. Mr. Tower thought at first that the Bible was Father's, but it wasn't. It has your name in the front cover." She ran to get the Book.

Katie's hands shook. "It—it is my Bible. The one Jordan had borrowed. Where did Mr. Tower find it?"

"It was with the other confiscated items."

"It must have been stolen from Jordan. He's probably out looking for it."

Jennifer shrugged. "One wishes that Book could talk. We'll probably never know the story it could tell. But I'm glad you got it back before you have to leave for New York."

Katie opened the Bible slowly, hoping to find some message from Jordan tucked inside. There was none. Her last hope of seeing Jordan again faded.

Mrs. Ellis Shelby. That's what she would have to write in the front of her Bible in just a few days. She felt chilled, and it wasn't even cold.

Chapter 16

APPRISING THE JUDGE

A copy of the new land laws lay on the table in front of Judge Stanley. He had studied them until his eyes blurred. He needed a diversion and decided on a brisk walk.

He was surprised to meet Harold Tower as he exited the hotel.

"There you are. I came to talk with you," the constable called. His face was tense, his words tight.

"Shall we go up to my room?"

"Somewhere private."

"What has happened, Harold? Has our village been raided? Is my family safe?"

"We buried Deacon Solomon yesterday."

"A great community loss."

When Mr. Stanley closed the heavy oak door behind them, the lawman crumbled into a chair. "We're supposed to be strong, Judge, but this case is getting to me. It hit too close to home."

"As bad as it is, Harold, all of us must face death at one time or another."

"Not like Matthew Solomon did!"

"What type of accident did he meet with?"

"It was no accident, Judge. It was cold murder!"

"Murder!"

"Let me start from the time you left. You had scarcely gotten out of town when Mr. Snyder's daughter came into town almost hysterical. She'd gone to check on her father and found the old man bound hand and foot. Whoever robbed him took all the savings he had and fled. The old fellow is nearly blind, and that precluded any description of the villains, but he said there were several of them."

"No clues?"

"Not a clue. But that's not all. Mrs. Moore's house was hit about a week later. Fortunately, she heard them coming and hid. She lost all her valuables and didn't get a good look at any of the robbers. I still had nothing to go on.

"Then last Friday, Matthew Solomon was murdered—"

"At his home?"

"No, that's one of the quirks of the case. He and Mark had started to Montana to help John build a cabin. They'd gone about fifty miles and were camped. While Mark was gone to gather wood, Mr. Solomon was mugged and his horse taken. He was drawing his dying breath when Mark returned."

"Bandits. The hard kind to track."

"No, now you're getting ahead of me. I'm trying to keep everything in chronological order for you so you'll understand it when the case comes to trial."

"My apologies, Harold. Go ahead."

"On Sunday, the murderer came boldly riding downtown on Mr. Solomon's horse—"

"You don't say!"

"Wait until you hear this: *and wearing Mr. Solomon's clothes!* I spotted him the minute he came onto Main Street."

"Did he try to outdistance you?"

"No. He wasn't even armed, offered no resistance, and claimed absolute innocence. He didn't get smart with me. In fact, he was the epitome of politeness. His lies were so convincing, it unnerved me. But there was all the evidence. He even had our last Sunday's collection report in his pocket and carried a Bible!"

"Mr. Solomon's Bible?"

"No. I checked it out and the Bible belonged to the Matterhorn girl. I can't imagine how he got it."

"You don't suppose he was framed?"

"I checked his story out with the references he gave."

"He knew someone in Greenfield?"

"He'd been living with a couple of transients out in the old Barnes house. None of his statements matched up with theirs. He claimed they bought the horse and he borrowed it and the clothes to go to church."

"That would border on blasphemy, wouldn't it, Harold?"

"Made me feel creepy."

"What did the references say?"

"They said they suspicioned all along that he'd been up to mischief. He lost his horse on a trip they were making to see relatives and needed another. He left them—and came back with a black horse. He also came back with blood-splattered clothes."

"Sounds like you have your man. Is he in our jail now?"

"No—"

"Don't tell me he escaped!"

"Feelings are running so rampant in Greenfield, Judge, that I deemed it wise to take him out of town for safekeeping. I took him to Stafford. That jail has a good reputation of holding onto convicts."

"A wise decision. The murderer didn't try to break away from you?"

"Not once."

"What was his name?"

"J. Thomasor."

"An assumed name, no doubt."

"It makes no difference. He'll hang with one name the same as he'd hang with another."

"Of course, I'm distressed that a chance passerby chose our town for his crime."

"He tried to throw me off on his intended destination, too. He said he'd started through to California for work, but the two men I interviewed said they were headed for Colorado—that their plans had never included California."

"I suppose the Solomons are taking it badly."

"We're all taking it badly. When I stopped by the Solomons to return Mr. Solomon's clothing—and the Bible that the young Miss Solomon offered to return to her friend—they told me a story that makes me angry enough to join a lynching mob myself!"

"Tell me, Harold."

"The brute who committed the murder went flaunting himself by the Solomons' house on Sunday morning riding Mr. Solomon's horse and garbed in his clothes. He even doffed Mr. Solomon's hat to the daughter as she stood on the front porch. She thought he was going to stop, dismount, and attack her, too! He purposefully and willfully terrified her so badly that she has been ill."

"It sounds unthinkable."

"I wish it had been. But unfortunately, the murderer thought it all up. Every morbid detail."

"What does he look like?"

"A handsome chap. Said he was twenty-one, claimed it was his birthday. Rich head of hair, broad shoulders— perfect specimen of manhood. I'd never have picked him for a criminal from any lineup. He's not afraid to look you straight in the eye and lie, either. That's why I felt that I had to talk with you. Greenfield is clamoring for a trial, and I don't trust anybody to handle this case but you. This is no run-of-the-mill case."

"I'm just finishing up here. We'll get the final amendments to these land laws tomorrow. The information I have obtained excites me so that I can hardly sleep, Harold. I'm afraid I'll miss history in the making! The oil boom is headed our way, and with the railroad stretched across our territory, we're on the verge of a great economic development. And what I like is that our laws include provisions for initiative and referendum. But I should be home this week, and we can proceed with the trial."

"Good. The news will give some relief to Greenfield's tension. We'll await your arrival to schedule the time."

Mr. Tower left and the judge picked up his strewn sheets and arranged them neatly in his portmanteau. He would be glad to get home and feel the heartthrob of his community again. Their troubles were his troubles. Another day and he would be headed that way. . . .

The Other Side of Jordan

Judge Stanley slipped on the stairwell that evening and broke his ankle. It would delay his going home, the doctor said, by several days. Or maybe weeks.

Chapter 17

THE UNLOCKED CELL

For Jordan Thomas, the days were long, the nights longer. He wished that his trial might be over and he could welcome his fateful end.

Katie's face came to him in nightmarish dreams. Always she had tears in her eyes because she had lost her beloved Bible. It haunted him. If he could have returned the loan, his mind would be at rest. He shouldn't have taken it, but she insisted. For her sake, he wished he had never walked out of her parlor with it; for his sake, he was glad he did.

Katie had talked to him about One who could patch a torn heart and marked some verses of Scripture for him. Since that day, much construction had gone on in his life. His heart was still in need of patching, but his soul seemed brand-new.

The deputy made frequent checks on Jordan. Taciturn at first, he made small conversation with his prisoner as time went on. One hot day, he stopped by the iron-latticed cubicle. "I didn't get many details of your crime," he said.

"You have been a model prisoner, and I find it hard to believe that you deliberately killed a man. Was it perhaps an accident or an act of self-defense?"

"Neither." Jordan held his head high. "I am accused of a crime that I did not commit, sir." There was no rancor in his voice.

"Want to talk about it?"

"I don't know anything about the crime."

"How is it that you were in a position to be accused of murder?"

"I joined up with three men; I shouldn't have. The leader told me that they were going through to California for work in the mines, and he offered to provide me with transportation there. I was out of a job at the time and saw it as an opportunity to better myself."

"These three men—what were they like?"

"I didn't learn much about them, sir. They were not my kind, I was not theirs. Therefore, I kept my attention off them as much as possible. Flynn, the leader, was a short, stocky man beginning to bald around his forehead. He was cold-blooded, heartless. Pete was an unscrupulous yes man for the leader. He had a nasty scar across his face. Lucky was dark and swarthy. He seemed less violent than the other two."

"Go on with your story."

"They said when I joined them that there would be some petty stealing just for food on the way to the West Coast. As it turned out, there were burglaries and they took more than salt pork. It made me sick-hearted. Although I never robbed anyone myself, I stood guard and took whatever they doled out to me, both in food and money. I hated every dime they gave me; I was wrong to take anything. Better had I starved. I did plan, though, to pay it back. I decided to break away, but the leader of the outfit kept me under threat of my life.

"They left Greenfield on Thursday, the twelfth day of May, to intercept a caravan they heard was headed back east with gold. I didn't go."

"Why didn't you leave while they were gone?"

"I was tempted to do just that, sir. But I'd given my word that I wouldn't. That's the only way they would consent for me to stay behind. When I give my word, it's settled.

"While they were gone, I checked stagecoach schedules. I had decided to leave when they returned, whatever Flynn's reaction. The coach was due through Monday.

"Two of the three men returned on Saturday night after dark. They told me they had bought a black horse to replace one that washed down river on their trip. They offered me free use of the horse as well as the clothing in the saddlebag.

"When I started to church on Sunday morning wearing the clothes and riding the horse they claimed to have purchased, I was apprehended and brought here."

The jailer waited for more. "And that's it?"

"That's it."

"So what do you make of the whole incident?"

"I can only surmise that those unprincipled men must have stolen the horse and done away with the owner. Knowing them as I do, you can be sure that I will be the scamp and take the clobbering for whatever crime they committed." He shifted on the hard slab. "I realize now that's why they took me on. But I'll not be the first man to be hanged by mistake, nor will I be the last. Even

Christ, my perfect example, was killed unjustly for the sins of others."

"What happened to the third man you mentioned?"

"Lucky? Flynn and Pete said he deserted them."

"And you think these men will witness against you at trial?"

"If they don't skip out before then."

"Mr. Thomasor, I believe what you have told me. Your story has an honest ring to it. But since I wasn't there, I have no proof that you're telling the truth. My gut feeling won't help when it comes hanging time. However, I will do anything I can for you as long as you are here. If you'll give me the address of your family, I'll contact them. It may be that they can come up with a good defense attorney or some clue to prove your innocence."

"I have no family, sir."

"None at all?"

"None. And that's good, since my life has come to this. There'll be no mother to grieve, no father to mourn my passing. Of that I can be thankful."

"You're not afraid to die?"

"No, sir."

"Thomasor, you're a unique man."

"A few weeks ago, death was a terror to me, but I've had a change in my life."

"I—I don't understand. Most of my prisoners on death row curse and rant and fight death. It's almost as if you—welcome it."

"I borrowed a Bible from a—a friend and read it for the better part of two days. I learned that this body—" he thumped his chest—"is only a temporary residence for the soul. I've never had anything but heartaches on this

144

earth, and the higher world of tearless eyes and mansions seems the better place to be." Jordan chuckled. "Even if I have to be pulled into heaven with a rope around my neck." He paused for reflection. "I've had some good talks with the Builder and Maker of the land beyond lately."

The deputy turned his face away. "Then is there anything else I might do for you?"

"I need to be baptized before I die."

"I'll see what I can do."

"Thank you."

"This friend you mentioned who lent you the Bible—could I contact him for you?"

"Her. Yes, her name is Katie Matterhorn. She lives near Greenfield. Just tell her I'm sorry about her Bible. Mr. Tower has it. I hope she will get it back."

"I'll see that she gets that message, Thomasor. Who knows, though," he winked, and there was an element of mystery in his wink, "you may see her before I do."

"I don't expect to ever see her again, sir."

"Do you know this country pretty well?"

"No, sir. I spent my life in a small area. I've never traveled much. Turned loose, I wouldn't even know how to get back to my birthplace without some directions."

"Rough country, there is, northwest of here." He gave his thumb a jerk. "Takes you off up into Colorado and there's a trail on out to Utah. A real no-man's-land. A body could get himself lost up that direction mighty easy."

"Are you thinking that the men who did the crime will disappear into that area?"

"I wasn't talking about them."

"About Lucky?"

"No."

The deputy said no more. He unlocked the cell and handed Jordan a loaf of bread. It smelled good. When he walked away, he did not lock the door back.

He wants me to escape, Jordan thought. *He left the door unlocked so that I can make a getaway. He even told me which direction to run. But I won't do it. Because if I did, I'd be a hunted man, always looking over my shoulder.*

He broke the bread off in chunks; it wasn't as good as Lydia Matterhorn's, but anything tasted good when one was hungry.

The Matterhorns. What would Katie's reaction be to the message the deputy promised to send her? Since no one except Flynn and Pete knew when or where the crime was committed, the scales were not tilted in Jordan's favor. Katie would have no reason to believe him innocent. He winced, suddenly realizing that he wanted her to believe—to know—that he was not guilty of murder.

The guard didn't return that day. For all those hours, Jordan was a free man if he wanted to be. He supposed that the man was trying to give him time to put a good distance between the jail and the wilderness of which he spoke before anyone "discovered" the escape.

I may die, Jordan told himself, *but I will not die a coward.* He would not die running from the law. If he made his break, Katie would always remember him as an outlaw, a fugitive. Death would be more honorable.

Even now, Jordan knew that if he could look into Katie's violet eyes and tell her that he did not commit the crime, she would believe him. *If only he could. . . .* But of course, he would not have that chance.

When the jailer returned the next morning, Jordan was asleep on his bench. How long the guard stood and watched him, he did not know. But some noise, some movement, roused him and he immediately sat up.

"You forgot to lock the door yesterday when you left my cell, sir," he said.

The deputy put on a pretense of surprise. "Did I? That was very careless of me, wasn't it? I almost broke my record. A man could lose his job for less than that. When did you discover my mistake?"

"As soon as you left." He grinned. "Anyone could have gotten into my house at any time during the night and kidnapped me, sir!"

"Why didn't you take advantage of my error and make your break? I'm sure you are the only prisoner I ever had who wouldn't."

"Would that have been honest of me, sir?"

"A body will do a lot to save himself from the noose, honest or dishonest."

"Sir, it isn't my body I'm seeking to save, it is my soul. Had I left, you would always have questioned my integrity. You said yourself that you have no proof that I am clean. To have you—and others—remember me as a deserter would be worse than the death sentence itself."

"You're a unique man, Thomasor." The deputy locked the door and walked away.

147

Chapter 18

CONFUSING MESSAGE

K atie pulled the thread through the needle's eye and secured a knot in the end of it. She had coaxed thousands of tiny stitches into the wedding dress, and yet there were thousands to go—and time was running out. It seemed to take much longer to do a thing when one's heart lagged behind. She examined her handiwork. Jordan Thomas once commented on the lovely stitches she made. Would Ellis Shelby even notice—or care?

Katie had wanted a small wedding in the sitting room here at home with just her mother and father and the parson. But Lydia and Jennifer insisted she must have a church wedding. Jennifer wrote a song; Mrs. Solomon suggested a bouquet of roses. So Katie let them have their way with the planning.

Another letter came from Cynthia. Ellis was on his way. There was a grand party announced to celebrate her arrival in New York, Cynthia said, after which the newlyweds would be on their way to a lavish honeymoon in some

149

foreign country.

Katie frowned. It seemed to her that God had been left out of all the plans. Cynthia again ignored the questions concerning Ellis's spiritual status. It became obvious that her aunt purposely sidestepped any discussion of religion in connection with Ellis: where he attended church, his commitment, his love for truth and right.

Katie had mentioned this to her mother, but Lydia said it was surely an oversight on Cynthia's part. One couldn't remember to answer all questions in a long-distance correspondence.

Katie stared out the window, her mind turning over the threadbare worry. Her hands lay idle and listless in her lap.

Her eyes caught a movement. It was her father hurrying through the iron gate and down the path, his face a study. What was wrong? She tossed the wedding dress into a heap on her bed and ran to meet him. "What is it, Father?"

He said nothing until he was inside and had pulled the door shut behind him. "Lydia. Katie. Matthew Solomon's murderer has been caught."

"Oh, thank God! We prayed that he would be," cheered Lydia. "It is an answer to our prayers. Now the Solomons won't have to live in constant fear. Poor things, they bolt their doors and windows every night. Where did they finally find the man, Maynard?"

"I have few actual facts. Most of the rumors are hearsay. You know how close-mouthed Mr. Tower is. He knows the details, but he's not talking. They say he's afraid of a lynching."

"How did you find out about it?"

"A jailer who would not give his name or tell where he was from was sent to me."

"Sent to you?"

"Yes. He was trying to locate Katie."

Katie let her body sink into a nearby chair for support. "Why was he trying to find me?"

"He said the man who is in jail for the murder asked him to get a message through to you."

"But—I don't understand, Father. I wouldn't know the murderer."

"No, we don't know him. I told the jailer as much. And after you hear the message the criminal sent to you, you'll likely be more confused than ever." He consulted a note on which he had scribbled details so as not to forget. "Let's see here. I jotted the message down to get it exact. . . . The convict sends his apologies about your Bible and said he hoped you got it back."

"I got my Bible back, Father."

"Where was your Bible?"

"I loaned it to Jordan Thomas, remember?"

"Oh, yes, I remember. But how did you get it back? Jordan hasn't—"

"Mr. Tower took it to the Solomons along with the other recovered items from the robbery, and Jennifer returned it to me. Jennifer and I have a notion that Jordan Thomas must have lost it or had it stolen from him."

"The murderer wasn't a local man."

"Who would steal a Bible?" Lydia looked from her daughter to her husband for an explanation.

Mr. Matterhorn bunched his shoulders. "I am no less baffled than you are, Lydia. A Bible and a killing don't pair up. Killing someone while carrying a Bible that says

'Thou shalt not kill' would seem ironic to me."

"Does Mr. Tower think the man who killed Brother Solomon might be the one who tied old Mr. Snyder up and took the Moores' savings?"

"He's not talking. Old Mr. Snyder is so poorly, they don't expect him to live. He'll not be able to witness at the trial."

"If Mr. Snyder dies, that would constitute another charge against the criminal, wouldn't it?"

"I should think it would."

"A hanging in Greenfield—do you think it will happen, Maynard?"

"I think it will. An offense can't get much worse. Men have been hanged for a lot less."

"Will the trial be right away?"

"They're waiting for Judge Stanley to get back. He had planned to return this week, but we've just heard that he met with an accident and broke his foot. Nobody seems to know how long it'll take him to recover."

"Can't they appoint someone to do his work and get on with the trial?"

"They could, but Mr. Tower thinks no one can make a right and proper decision but Judge Stanley. They've worked together for years. My guess is that nothing will be done until the honorable judge gets back to his post of duty, whatever his duration of absence."

"But Maynard! The man could *escape.*" Her voice rose to a high pitch. "A blind judge could see that this convict is guilty. Jennifer saw the man herself, riding on Charley Horse and wearing Matthew Solomon's suit."

"And carrying my Bible!" Katie's indignation spilled out. "Such a vile man holding something so holy!"

Lydia shook her head as if to clear it. "Did no one learn the man's name or his whereabouts, Maynard?"

"His name is Jay Tomsor. No one in Greenfield has ever heard the name before. And no one seems to know why he was in town the day Jennifer saw him."

"What age is he?" Lydia asked. "Did they say?"

"He's old enough to be a hardened criminal."

"Why any man would want to rob and kill someone as kind-hearted as Mr. Solomon is a mystification within itself."

"Rumor has it that he rode directly into the heart of Greenfield as if daring the constable to arrest him. And now word has leaked out that he is claiming absolute innocence in the crime with all the hard evidence against him." Mr. Matterhorn let out his breath in a sound of exasperation. "The man must be possessed of a legion of evil spirits."

"My name is in the front of my Bible." Katie blanched. "So now the killer knows my name!"

"What confounds me is why a murderer would be so concerned whether or not your Bible was ever returned to you, Katie. I can't—"

The door knocker clanked abruptly. Katie jumped. Mr. Matterhorn motioned for silence as he opened the door a small crack and reached beside it for his shotgun. Then he flung it back for Jennifer Solomon.

"Come on in, Jennifer." Katie gave a nervous laugh.

"Why is everyone so quiet? Is someone ill?"

"Father just brought me a strange message and we're all high-strung."

Alarm widened Jennifer's eyes. "Danger?"

"I hope not. The convict who brought so much grief

153

to your family just sent me a message."

"You a message?"

"Yes. By a jailer. He made apologies about my Bible and said he hoped that I would get it back."

"That's all?"

Mr. Matterhorn nodded.

"He didn't apologize for the murder? Or for stealing Charley Horse? Or for wearing Father's clothes? Or for tormenting us?"

Katie looked to her father for Jennifer's answers.

"Nothing," Mr. Matterhorn said. "Nothing except the Bible."

"He's a stranger that none of us know, Jennifer. The jailer gave Father the man's name. It's Jay Tomsor. From all accounts, he did the deed for sport, then dared Mr. Tower to arrest him. He must be a very wicked man. But, of course, he will get his just reward when Judge Stanley gets home."

"I had so much bitterness at first, Katie. I wanted revenge. Then I—I prayed for the poor man's soul. And now I feel a certain peace." Jennifer's face was soft. "Once you told me that God could patch torn hearts. That's what He's doing for me now. We know that Father is in a better place, a place he talked a lot about." She gave a high-priced smile. "Come on, let's get to work on your wedding dress. I've come to help you. I've only a few more days to be with you before you get rich and famous and forget all about me!"

Mr. Matterhorn left the room abruptly, his footsteps heavy.

154

Chapter 19

CHANCE MEETING

Somewhere in Missouri, Ellis Shelby picked up a traveler. Bored with his trained servants—a valet and the coach driver—he thought the hillbilly would be an amusing diversion. Ellis welcomed diversions of any sort.

His father and Cynthia would not approve of his taking in the stranger, especially with as much money as he had in his possession, but Ellis felt a sensuous delight in breaking rules. He always kept rebellion within his beck and call.

The wayfaring man's name was Todd. "De-sided it wuz time I toddled out an' seeked me fortune," the man punned, slapping his knee with a rawboned hand.

Ellis guessed that Todd hovered around mid-life. Sprigs of gray seeded out in his mop of rust-colored hair. His eyes seemed tie-dyed to match wiry brown brows. His mountain idioms entertained and fascinated the city-bred Ellis.

Todd had started, he told Ellis, to the plains of Texas "whar round weeds chopped tharselves off at th' stalks

an' went tumblin' all over th' world spreadin' seeds." He
called them "tumblin' weeds." He'd always "hankered"
to see one, he allowed, wondering why one had never
bothered to tumble to Missouri—and then answering
himself that they must have "drowned" trying to get
across the Arkansas River "like Pharaoh went to Davy
Jones's locker in th' Red Sea." Todd did a lot of thinking
out loud, a lot of asking and a lot of answering.

His real objective, though, he said, was to try to find
some of his "lost an' homely" cousins "scattered worser'n
them thar weeds." To hear him tell it, he had "dozens
an' dozens o' cuzins" that made up a great percent of the
world's population.

When a light shower fell while the sun was shining,
Todd said, "No need wonderin' what th' devil's doin' with
hisself t'day; he's a-whippin' 'is wife!"

"Why would he do that, Mr. Todd?" Ellis spurred him
on.

"That's whut it means when it rains an' suns at th'
same time. An' shore, thar'll be rain agin tomorry." He
grinned over at Ellis. "Course we'll be rollin' on down
th' road uprunnin' that thar rain."

The driver and the valet threw scornful looks at Todd.
Their scowls censured Ellis for giving the uncouth man
transportation in the mayor's expensive coach. But
neither Ellis nor Todd gave attention to their reproaches.
Ellis took perverse pleasure in provoking them. It was
a part of the game.

When Todd learned that Ellis made the trip to meet
his future bride, he poked at Ellis with joshing advice.
"Is she purty?"

"Am I handsome?" countered Ellis.

"In an ugly sort o' way."

"She's ugly in a pretty sort of way."

"She musta swallowed aplenty o' raw chicken hearts whole. Ozarkers 'llow that's what brings on good looks in dames."

"Were you born and reared in the Ozarks, Mr. Todd?"

"Rared? You mean raised?"

"Yes."

"That I wuz, sonny. My old grandpap wuz th' smartest man in them thar hills on charms an' haints. He'd'a done fine, they say, hadn't it been fer Grandmam. She dis-believed his believes.

"It wuz 'er purty that be-guiled Grandpap. Ever'body avowed she was docterin' up 'er cheeks with red sap from them cow-slobber weeds. But Grandpap knowed she didn't hold with paint an' put-on. Her collerin' wuz jest as natur'l as th' curl in a pig's tail.

"Now you know, don't ye, Mr. Ellis, that on th' night o' yer weddin', yer bound an' determined to stay awake th' longest?"

"Why?"

"Cause it's th' one what goes to sleep first that dies first. Grandpap wadn't wantin' to be th' first to take to 'is coffin an' let some'un else have 'is purty. So's he waited til he wuz sure Grandmam wuz a-sleepin', then he let hisself t' slumber."

"Did she die first?"

Todd seemed to anticipate the question. "Why, no. She's still alive. Either she wuz jest pertendin' to be asleepin' or else 'er disbelief in 'is old mountain notions dispowered 'im to win."

A look akin to merriment played on his face. "Grand-

157

mam is a spunk."

Ellis liked the new word; it had a reckless sound to it.

"What be th' name o' th' bonnie yer broom-jumpin' with?"

"Katie Matterhorn."

He clapped his hands together. "Per-fect! Her last name can't front with th' same letter as yor'n. 'Change th' name an' not th' letter, marry fer worse an' not fer better.' "

The hillbilly, with his peculiar folklore, kept Ellis engrossed all the way to Greenfield. He rode in grand style at Ellis's expense.

"Wish me dozens an' dozens o' cuzins could see me in this high an' mighty buggy," he commented as Ellis brought the coach to a stop. "I never rid in nuthin' this cushy." He ran his fingers over the velvet seat. "But ain't nuthin' ever abashed me yet. All of us'ns er made out o' mud. Yep, just dirt. Uppity folks calls it *clay*. But it's all added up th' same. Some jest try to mix in a little ore."

"We're here."

Todd squinted. "Say, this here town looks plumb Ozarky. Good place to find a cuzin'."

Ellis, in all his majesty, took Greenfield by storm. The innkeeper's daughter lolled around the registration desk giving him wanton looks and later tittering to her school friends about the "rich and handsome man" at their lodge. "He's got a glad eye," she reported. "And you should see him step!"

The majority of the populace had never set sight on such an elegant carriage with gold couplings and red velvet curtains. Ellis himself enjoyed the rumpus he caused; he wore his silk top hat just to see the reaction of the commoners. Ellis liked attention.

He ordered the best possible accommodations, demanding preferential suites for his entire company, including Todd. Then he complained loudly about the inferior rooms, the poor service, and everything in general. "This is the rattiest place I've ever stayed," he griped. "Our stables in New York are cleaner than this."

"Why, this seems pert-nigh like heaven to me," Todd grinned, showing gaps where teeth should have been. "Where I come frum, they'd call this plushy."

The town bent over backwards to please Ellis. They learned that when Ellis was pleased, he passed out gratuities liberally. However, Ellis was seldom pleased with anything.

Word got out that the young "millionaire" had come to claim one of Greenfield's local maidens for his bride, and there were bets on who the girl might be. Some said it was doubtless the mayor's daughter, Idabelle Lester, a large top-heavy girl woefully lacking in physical beauty. Others said it might be the deceased deacon's daughter, Jennifer Solomon. She was a raven-haired beauty in her own rights. One or two mentioned Katie, but she didn't get many votes.

"The reason I think it might be Katie Matterhorn," a storekeeper said to a customer, "is because she has been buying yards and yards of lace. I'm thinking she may have bought it for the making of her trousseau."

"But the Matterhorns are poor," objected the customer. "And they say this young man is very wealthy. I wouldn't think Miss Matterhorn his type."

"Poor they are, but gossip has it that Lydia Matterhorn has a rich relative up north."

159

"Could be."

"Whoever his fortunate lady, he doesn't seem anxious to court her, does he? He's been here for two days now and nobody has seen him in the company of any young lady."

"I saw him talking to the innkeeper's daughter."

"Surely he wouldn't want her!" She lowered her voice. "With her reputation!"

Ellis was in no hurry to jeopardize his freedom. Word reached Katie that he was in town, but he did not call on her. Their meeting was, in fact, quite by accident.

On Saturday, Ellis put on his best suit with tails and the silk top hat and walked down the boardwalk parading the arrogance woven into the fiber of his character. He wished to see and be seen. As his eyes darted from girl to girl, he recognized a familiar face. He had seen that hair, those eyes, that profile, in Cynthia's picture. This was Katie Matterhorn.

The girl started to dart into a store and caught her heel. When she tottered, he grabbed her arm and jerked her back roughly. "I think you are the young lady I have come to Greenfield to see."

Her eyes challenged him. "You must be Ellis Shelby. I heard that you were in town."

"*Mr.* Ellis Shelby." He bowed, making sure everyone on the walkway saw him. "And you, of course, are Katie Matterhorn." His glance swept across her plain dress with open scorn. "I had hoped that you would be dressed more appropriately for our first meeting. How is it that you came out in public wearing *that?*" His lip curled.

"I—I didn't know I would—would meet you—Mr. Ellis Shelby," she said. Ellis took sadistic pleasure in her discomfort.

"I prefer to acknowledge you publicly when you are more prepared, Miss Matterhorn. It will save embarrassment for both of us. Can you meet me at the inn tomorrow?"

"Oh, no sir! I'll be at church tomorrow. You will please worship with my family and me there, won't you? And then—and then have dinner with us afterwards. Mother will be delighted to serve you, I'm sure."

"Church?" He lifted his well-shaped chin and gave a loud laugh that could be heard across the street. Men stopped to listen; women turned. "I haven't been in a church since the day I was christened Ellis Quincy Shelby. It's a bit late for me to start being churchy now, don't you think?"

"It's never too late to live for God." She barely whispered it.

"Live for God?" Now he lowered his voice for her ears only. "I live for Ellis Shelby, my dear lady. Your aunt warned me that you overdo religion. But we'll work on that later. Go on to your chapel. There'll be plenty of time for us to meet and make our arrangements for the wedding next week.

"And when we have our conference, I want it to be in the tearoom of the inn. Cynthia tells me that your house is rather small and unaccommodating for guests. I'd prefer to talk with you in a more solicitous setting. We could go up to my room after we've had something to drink. I'll meet your parents later on when you and I have become better acquainted." He gave a lustful wink.

"I hope you have a good day, Mr. Shelby." They were frost-bitten words.

"Oh, I will." He was flippant. "I'm rather enjoying

161

the primitive parties at the outmoded roadhouse. I wish I had had this experience before I wrote my college thesis on medieval habiliments. I would have made the top grade in my class!"

Katie looked at him, unsmiling.

"And I was about to forget. Your aunt sent your wedding dress and the veil. I hope it is yet in good repair. I told my valet to see to its safety. You may call for it at the inn anytime. Culpepper will get it for you."

"I'll send Father to fetch it."

"*Fetch* it?" He shrugged. "As you will." Then, seeing the innkeeper's daughter coming his direction, he made a quick getaway so that she would not see him talking to Katie dressed in her peasant costume.

Ellis Shelby was ill-tempered the rest of the day. He snapped at his footman. He slammed doors, kicked furniture.

"What's eating on you, Mr. Ellis?" Culpepper asked the question at the risk of a tongue-lashing. "These uncultured heathens getting on your nerves?"

"That's about what it amounts to, Culpepper."

"I think we should go back to New York, sir. No girl from this illiterate hinterland could adapt to our world. You'd be wise to choose a lady from your own social class. There's plenty to choose from up there."

"Cynthia Goldstein says we can cultivate her niece."

"You can't."

"You may be wisdom's child, Culpepper. I'm sick to death of this place. All I hear on the streets, in the business houses, everywhere is about the murder of one of their sainted deacons. Mr. Solomon did this and Mr. Solomon did that. He was obviously an archangel. They can't give me proper service for their obsession with a dead bishop."

"I'm hearing it myself, sir."

"I would say we'll do ourselves a favor to start back for civilization Monday. And that'll be none too soon to suit me. Get us ready."

"You'll have to tell the girl you've backed out on the wedding."

Ellis hooted. "I'm Ellis Shelby, Culpepper. I don't have to account to any bumpkin of a girl. The mayor's son kowtowing to a peon! Ha! I can drive off without saying a word to her. Or anybody. It's my privilege. And I'll do just that!"

"It'll be Mrs. Goldstein you'll have to account to when you get back to New York."

"I'll have miles and miles between here and there to author a very credible story, won't I?"

Culpepper nodded. "Yes, sir."

"In the meantime, I'm near to going mad as a hatter with boredom. Isn't there anything we can do for a bit of entertainment? I'd like to see the raw side of this town."

"Mr. Todd is going to the gambling house this evening. You can't get much lower than that. But it's a good place to lose your money."

"I'm not afraid of losing money," Ellis said carelessly. "I think I'll go along with old Todd."

"You wouldn't stand a chance in a game against the sharks that will be there," reminded Culpepper.

"I'll give Todd some money—and sit back and watch. That would beat another dry party here where they serve nothing stronger than *lemonade!*"

163

That night, Ellis went to the den of iniquity with Todd. But just before he left, Katie's father came by to pick up the wedding dress that Cynthia Goldstein sent to her niece for her wedding.

Ellis sent Culpepper to the door with the dress. He did not wish to see Mr. Matterhorn.

HILLBILLY COUSIN

"**B**een waiting all week for today so I could go into town and double our money, Pete," Flynn said on Saturday.

"Thought I might go with you, boss."

"No, you stay here. You have a way of jinxing my good luck. We need some more money to last until that trial. Can't afford to get caught at any tricks betwixt now and then. Won't be able to take collections. Our only hope of a windfall is me winning at craps tonight."

"What if you lose what we've got?"

"That's why I'm leaving you home. So I won't. See, Pete, if I'm in town and you're here, I'll be far enough away that your tempting of fate won't affect me."

"I see, boss. I'll stay here if you say so."

"You stumbled over a log this morning, and stumbling over something first thing in the morning means ill luck all day."

"Is there any way to uncuss that?"

"Yes, but it's probably too late now. You should have

turned around three times."

Pete made three fast spins. "And say a rhyme?"

"Nothing for stumbling."

"Good. Some of those sayings don't make sense anyhow."

Flynn's fists tightened. "Are you saying that my grandpap didn't know what he was talking about?"

"Well, no," Pete stayed calm, matter-of-fact. "But yesterday you made me say 'bread and butter' when I passed on one side of the tree and you on the other. Why?"

"I don't know. It just breaks the spell."

"What spell?"

"The spell of something coming between us. And with the trial coming up, we can't have no divisions in our thinking."

Pete's eyes brightened. "I see the sense in it now, boss! Bread and butter *stick together!*"

Flynn picked up the bag that contained Jordan's money. "Don't expect me back early. What you start on a Saturday, you have to finish, be it a job or be it a game. If you don't, it'll be six Saturdays before you get it done."

"Then stay and finish, boss."

When Flynn walked into the gambling hall, it was crowded. This surprised him. He peered through the cosmos of cheap cigar smoke in the dimly lighted den to get a better look at the company gathered there.

He was pleased to see a prosperous-looking businessman with a silk top hat in his left hand. Silk top hats meant wealth; he'd seen few of them in his lifetime.

Beside the rich man sat a leather-faced fellow, apparent owner of a floppy-brimmed mountaineer's hat. The two, so diverse, conversed like brothers. The older man sat at the table with Gambler Bill while the "rich young ruler," as Flynn mentally labeled him, looked on. The man suddenly snapped his fingers and chanted: "Come seven, come eleven."

Involuntarily, Flynn's grimy fingers locked around the money in his pocket, as if to hold it from sure escape. With a sudden resolve, he decided not to play at all. Here was someone who knew all the magic words that Grandpap had used. Who was this stranger?

When Gambler Bill lost the game to the man called Todd, he invited Flynn to play. "I've got no money tonight, Bill," lied Flynn. "Work's been slow this week."

"What sort of work do you do?" the gambler asked.

"I make wagon tongues," Flynn said.

"About the same as my work," roared Bill. "I make tongues wag. Ain't much difference between a wagon tongue and a waggin' tongue. About the same length, I allow." He laughed at his own joke.

"Wag your tongue and acquaint me with this new man here," Flynn said, nodding toward Todd.

"Named Todd. From the Ozarks."

Flynn's alcohol-taxed eyes gleamed. "Why, we just might be kin!" he said. "I was Ozark born and bred myself."

"Might be," agreed Todd. "I got dozens an' dozens o' cuzins all over creation. I wuz thinkin' mayhap I'd run acrost two er one of 'um. Ever heared o' any Copelands?"

"That was my grandpap's name and you talk just like him!"

"Esque Todd Copeland?"

"He was my grandpap."

"Mine, too." They discovered that they were, indeed,

167

first cousins. "You got Grandmam's maiden name, ain't ye? She wuz a Flynn."

"Yep. But I'd rather been named for Grandpap. Grandmam was too holy-holy and she disbelieved Grandpap's luck charms."

"She did that awrighty! I wuz named for Grandpap." He blew on his fingernails. "That's why I won the craps game. It wuz 'is spirit playin'.'"

Flynn knew he'd found the man he wanted for his sidekick; here was a winner. "Where you headed?" he asked.

"I'm bound fer Texas t' see them flowers that wear th' blue bonnets on thar heads," Todd said. "Them thar hills of Missoury warn't makin' me no younger."

"You can travel along with us," Flynn invited, half afraid Todd would decline the offer. "It's just me and Pete now."

"I don't know nuthin' 'about makin' wagon tongues."

Flynn winked. "We've done gone out of business. Me and Pete are going to Colorado to get ourselves filthy rich."

"Or just filthy," put in Gambler Bill, tongue-in-cheek.

Flynn ignored him. "We'll be here awhile. There's a trial coming up that we both have to testify at. A boy that used to run with us stole a horse and killed the owner about fifty miles from here. We were almost eyewitnesses, and the law won't let us leave until we tell what we know. Then we can move on. We've been looking for a third man to replace one that deserted us. Three's a lucky number."

"I think I'll jest take ye up on thet, Cuzin Flynn!" Todd said. "I come this fer with Mr. Shelby frum New York, but he's plannin' on returnin' to New York next

week. Then I'll have no stayin' place. You have a camp-
in' place?''

"It isn't much."

"I cut me teeth on chitlins. I know how t' abound an'
I know how t' abase. Mr. Shelby has been treatin' me
kingish, but I'm used t' bein' treated beggarish as well."
Todd turned to Ellis. "Be awright with ye, sir, if I jest
move on in with me kissin' cuzin an' get outta yore way?"

Ellis nodded. "Suit yourself." He didn't take his eyes
off the game Gambler Bill played with another of his
cronies.

Flynn and Todd left the gambling hall together and
went to the inn for Todd's few belongings. "Ain't got
much, cuzin," Todd said.

"Runs in the family. I haven't either." Flynn let his
eyes slide around the room. "Are you sure you want to
leave this plushy stuff for a shack without windows?"

"I'm sure, Cuzin Flynn! I been sleepin' hot in this
windered place. Dirt floors an' cracks in th' walls would
make me feel more homeish."

"I'd be so everlasting scared of accidently seeing a
new moon through one of those fancy glasses that I'd take
stomach cramps," Flynn said. "I'd cover my eyes every
night."

"Now it's you what sounds jest like Grandpap!"

"Finding you is the best luck I've had this whole
moon." Flynn rubbed the back of his neck. "When I
sneezed on Thursday, I knew I was in for something better. You remember the sneezes, don't you?"

"Yep. Grandpap memorized 'em to me. Mondey is fer
danger, Tuesdey fer kissin' a stranger, Wednesdey fer
a letter, Thursdey fer somethin' better, Fridey fer sorrow,

169

Saturdey see a friend tomorry—an' Sundey . . . You remember Sundey, don't ye?"

"If you sneeze on Sunday, the devil will be with you all week. I do anything to keep from sneezing Sundays."

"You *real* superstitious?"

"Uh-huh."

"Travel by the moon signs?"

"Yep. Me and Pete have been anxious to heel out. We'd already been gone, but we're subpoenaed."

"What's that? It don't sound good."

"It's where the law says you have to show up to witness at a trial."

"I see."

"Now I'm glad we got held up until you came along. We needed a third party and you're our kind."

"Th' man up fer murder—he wuz yore kind?"

"We thought he was, Cousin, but we found out different. I'll pass it on to you just like it happened so you can stand and witness against him with me and Pete. We'll all join hands on this. The witness of three goes a lot better with a judge than the witness of two. And three are luckier, besides."

"I'll say what you say me to, jest so's you say it pure like it happened. I b'lieve in shootin' square with th' law. Always parked meself on th' right side of 'um. Never nighted in no hoosegow."

"We'll keep your nose clean, Todd. Trust us."

When the men came to the shack, Pete met them at the door. "Did you win for us, boss?"

"I won more than money, Pete! I got us the best man we've ever had in our pack. He's my own cousin from Missouri. He knows Grandpap's enchantments."

Pete's eyes glowed, then dulled. "You didn't lose our money, did you?"

"Not a penny. I didn't even play tonight. I left the playing up to Cousin Todd here. He won us some of Gambler Bill's stingy money!"

Todd pulled out a wad of money. "An' if'n we're here th' Saturday next, I'll go get us some more."

"He says, 'Come seven, come eleven,' Pete. That's why he wins."

"An' I snap."

"He's going to help us testify against Thomas at trial, Pete. That'll look better on our part. Three instead of two. Juries like numbers."

"But your cousin wasn't with us, boss."

"That's okay. We'll paint him up the picture so life-like, he'll think he was right there."

"You gotta paint right er th' colors will smear, Cuzin Flynn."

"It's the way you brush it on that counts." Flynn gave Pete a sly smile.

"Then after the trial, we'll be ready to hotfoot it to Colorado and the gold, won't we, boss?"

"You've got to do what I say at that trial, Pete, or we may never get to Colorado."

"I'll do anything you say, boss."

"So will I," Todd said. It was like a second echo, a little weaker than the first.

171

Chapter 21

USELESS DEFENSE

"**I**'ve heard all sorts of wonderful things about Ellis Shelby!" Jennifer gave Katie a squeeze. "I only wish that I might see him for myself. Where is he?"

"He's at the inn."

"Sadie, the innkeeper's daughter, says he is handsome to a fault! You've been spending a lot of time with him, I suppose?"

"Actually, I've—I've only seen him once." Flames of shame began in Katie's chest, sent a searing heat up her throat, and splashed thick burning color across her face. "I—I wasn't dressed properly, and I—I promised him that we would meet when I was more presentable."

"You're so self-conscious, Katie! I'm sure it didn't matter to him about your dress. Was he so good-looking?"

"I really didn't notice. Looks are of so little importance to me."

"But they are a great bonus. Why, everybody in town is talking about this Greek god!"

"His eyes aren't as nice as—that is, I didn't have much

opportunity to look directly at Ellis. It's unladylike to stare."

"If he was my beau and I'd never seen him, I'd stare."

"I'll have plenty of time for that. He said that we would get together next week to make our plans."

"You must be terribly excited!" Jennifer's eyes danced.

"I guess—it hasn't hit me yet."

"I was hoping Ellis would be here at church today and I'd have a chance to meet him."

"I mentioned it to him, but he said he'd—rather not attend."

Dark brows came up. "I guess he has his reasons, Katie. Maybe he's tired from his long trip. However, with a carriage so grand, one would think the ride would be as comfortable as sitting on goose-down pillows. They say his coach has red velvet curtains and gold trim. Have you seen your carriage?"

"No."

"It's like a fairytale and you the queen. I should think you would want to sneak by the inn just to get a peek at the chariot that will whisk you back to New York."

"There'll be plenty of time for that, too."

Jennifer caught Katie's arm and shook her. "Wake up, Katie! What is the matter with you? You are acting horrid."

Katie burst into tears. "Oh, Jennifer! I don't feel right inside about—about anything. Aunt Cynthia sent me a wedding gown that must have cost her a fortune. And I—I can't wear it!"

"Of course you can. Just because you had already made one doesn't mean—"

"But it's not *decent,*" she sobbed. "The neck is so low that it's—it's frightening. And the back is almost gone completely. Why, I'd feel naked in it. The parson certainly wouldn't wish anything so unholy inside the church."

"Stop blubbering, for heaven's sake, Katie. There's ways to fix anything. Fill it in with lace and satin; you're a good seamstress."

"Ellis would laugh, and Aunt Cynthia would be furious if I change the design."

"Ellis probably doesn't even know what it looks like! There's some rule of etiquette that a groom doesn't look at the dress before it's worn by his bride. What does your mother suggest?"

"She can't believe that Aunt Cynthia would send such a thing and expect me to wear it."

"They may have sent down the wrong gown. That does happen. Anyhow, we'll think of something. When is the wedding? How long do we have?"

"I don't know anything definite yet."

"I'm sure Ellis wishes to call on you formally and ask your father for your hand."

Katie turned her head away so that Jennifer could not divine the storm in her heart, afraid that misgivings shadowed her eyes. Even her best friend would not understand the inner turmoil. "He—said we'd talk this week."

Jennifer softened. "You'll feel better when it's all settled."

Each day passed in dread for Katie. She did not go to the inn as Ellis had proposed, and she feared he would come and demand of her a reason for her delinquency. She ate little, slept little. Lydia noticed.

"You are making yourself ill grieving for Ellis," her

The Other Side of Jordan

mother said. "He'll come calling by and by. Please try
to eat more. It won't be good for you as a new bride to
be sickly and weak for the trip back to New York."

"I don't think Ellis will come here, Mother." Katie
hesitated. "He asked me to meet him at the inn."

Lydia jumped up, agitated. "When?"

"Several days ago."

"Then, Katie, you should have gone immediately!
That was an invitation, and it was your duty to accept
it. You should have mentioned it sooner! Father would
have taken you in the wagon any day you asked."

"I have nothing proper to wear."

"What a silly thing to say! Starch and iron your best
gingham, wear a fresh collar and a bonnet, and you'll look
very fetching."

She could not bring herself to tell her mother that
Ellis had ridiculed her best dress. "And Ellis says he
wishes to see me alone."

"But of course! You are engaged. Sooner or later you
will be obliged to be alone with your bridegroom. I don't
understand a twenty-year-old who is so shy of a beau."

"But Ellis wants me to come to his room. Mother,
it isn't proper!"

"There will be others there. When Ellis said 'alone'
he didn't mean just the two of you in his bedchamber. The
man who delivered the wedding dress to your father will
be there."

"I'm not sure . . ."

"Katie, you can't sit here and disregard the request
of your espoused. You'll never get married at this rate.
I only wish I had known sooner. Now some apology will
needs be made on your part for the delay. What will Ellis

think?'' She untied her apron. "Oh, dear, what will Cynthia think?''

"If he loves me, he can come to my home!''

Her mother set her jaw, then mellowed to a child-placating tone. "Unfortunately, dear, we don't know the customs of the learned and the polished. We're mere country folk. In their culture, it probably is not proper for an educated man to call on a lady in the country first.''

Katie's face flushed. "He asked me to come for tea.''

"See? He wants it to be formal, not a house call. We can only hope that he forgives you. I hope he can look over the social blunder you've made. Certainly you must go to him at once.''

"I won't go alone.''

"Then your father and I will go with you and wait while he talks with you privately. Now hurry! Get yourself dressed and your hair crimped so that we'll be ready to leave when your father comes in from the field.''

Katie went to her room. Dark-circled and sunken eyes that had lost their luster looked back at her from the warped mirror. A crack in the looking glass broke her forehead into two parts. *A paradox,* she thought. *I should be thinking only of Ellis but my heart is with Jordan.* At the thought of Jordan, she smiled, but the contorted double turned her smile to a grimace.

Ellis's scornful laugh came back to dig trenches in her soul. Snatches of his proud talk washed over her in waves, each adding momentum. *Church . . . you overdo religion . . . we'll take care of that . . . you came out in public wearing that? . . .*

Her whole being shrank from meeting the scoffer again. The places he had injured still smarted. Why couldn't he have the same gentle eyes, the humility, the character of Jor—

"Are you ready, Katie?"

She reached for the button hook to fasten her shoes. "Almost, Mother."

On the townward trip, Mr. Matterhorn seemed grave, pensive. Sensing the strain, Katie's mother tried to fill the vacuous silence with idle pratter. "We can repair the wedding dress Cynthia sent with the fine English lace from my own wedding dress," she suggested.

"I shouldn't want to disfurnish your keepsake, Mother."

"Speak nothing of it. It's a small pittance for your happiness. Don't you agree, Maynard?"

He kept his eyes straight ahead. "Katie's happiness is my happiness, Lydia."

"He's dreading to lose you, Katie."

"I expected Mr. Shelby to come to meet me in person when I went to call for the wedding dress," Mr. Matterhorn said. "I should think he would like to see what sort of father-in-law he is getting."

"It was proper for him to send a servant down with the dress, Maynard. He's careful not to do anything that is improper. This is a small town, and people talk."

"I hope he will be even more careful in the future." His words were clipped.

"I think it delightful—and romantic—that he has asked Katie to the tearoom for their formal engagement. He probably has a bethrothal gift for her. That will give Greenfield something to talk about."

"The whole town is already talking."

"That's wonderful! Cynthia will be pleased—"

"Not so wonderful, I'm afraid. Ellis was seen going into old Bill's gambling room Saturday night."

"How could he tell one business place from another, Maynard? He's new to Greenfield. I'm sure he wandered into the hall quite by mistake."

"He could have asked anyone in town the nature of the place. And if it was a mistake, it took him a long time to realize his error. He should have politely excused himself at once when he discovered where he was."

"I'm sure that's what he did."

"He didn't. He stayed until the rowdy place closed down sometime in the wee morning hours of the Lord's Day. His valet had to carry him from the place, he'd had so much to drink."

"And where, Maynard, did you hear that vicious gossip? I've never known you to talebear. I knew the local girls were jealous, but I certainly never dreamed they'd stoop so low as to resort to pure character defamation. I can't—"

"Calm yourself, Lydia. The facts can be documented by Mr. Tower himself. Had not Mr. Culpepper taken personal charge of your future son-in-law and paid his substantial fine, he would be sitting in jail yet."

Katie held back from retching. She asked that her father please take her home, pleading illness. But Lydia said they must talk with Ellis before passing hasty judgment. "Nothing is cut so thin that it doesn't have two sides," she reminded. "He's in a strange town among strangers. Gambler Bill may have tricked him."

She persisted in her defense. "Cynthia said Ellis was a fine gentleman, and I'm sure her evaluation is correct. She has known him all his life. If Gambler Bill intoxicated

179

the boy and led him into money-losing games, he should be the one locked up! It wouldn't be the first boy he's conned."

Mr. Matterhorn said nothing more, and the silence weighed heavy. Katie's tears, restrained on the outside, fell inside and threatened to drown her heart. How could she bear more hurts?

At the inn, Mr. Matterhorn helped Katie from the wagon, then lifted Lydia down. He escorted them to the lobby where the innkeeper's daughter gave Katie a curious, pitying look.

"We've come to call on Mr. Ellis Shelby." Mr. Matterhorn stood straight; Katie was proud of her father.

"Mr. Shelby? I'm afraid he isn't here, sir." The innkeeper spoke up.

"When is he expected back?"

"He didn't say."

"We'll wait." Mr. Matterhorn looked around for chairs.

"I'm afraid you misunderstood me, sir," the man said. "Mr. Shelby has vacated his room and is gone. You may wait a lifetime."

"Do you know where he went?"

The innkeeper's daughter smirked. "He went back to New York where he came from. He said he was tired of this primitive place and all the talk of murder."

"When did he leave?"

"He's been gone for four days. He left Monday morning."

"Did he leave a message for Miss Katie Matterhorn?"

"He left no message at all."

"Some emergency has called him away," whispered

Lydia. She turned to pat Katie's hand. "Don't worry, dear, Ellis will be back. Someone must have sent a wire—"

"He didn't mention when he would be returning?" Mr. Matterhorn asked the question once more.

"He mentioned nothing at all about returning here. Good day, sir."

Katie stepped outside and pulled fresh air into her lungs. She felt as though she hadn't breathed in a week.

Chapter 22

DEATH IN THE NIGHT

W hen Ellis returned to his home, he found the place padlocked, the hired servants gone. "Father!" he called. "Let me in!" He pounded on the door. No one answered.

"I cannot imagine where the honorable mayor would be," the chauffeur pondered. "Unless there's a big political campaign somewhere."

"Why would everyone be gone?" Culpepper frowned. "The cook, the gardener, the housekeeper . . ."

Ellis's temper flared. He spun a verbal mile of oaths. "I'll get in!" he bellowed. "I'll kick the door down!"

Culpepper took over as he usually did when Ellis showed his immaturity. "Your father will be livid if you ruin his front door, Mr. Ellis. Please refrain yourself." He took Ellis by the arm. "Mrs. Goldstein will know where the honorable mayor is. We'll inquire of her."

Ellis took one last kick at the lead-glass door and ordered the driver to Cynthia's house. That was when he remembered that he had thought of no excuse for leaving Katie behind. His mind grabbed for a thread to weave a plausable story.

Cynthia met him at the door, all smiles. "My new nephew! Please do bring Katie on in. I'm so anxious to see her after all these years. I can hardly contain myself! And I'm so sorry, Ellis about your father's heart failure—"

"Heart failure?"

"You didn't know?"

"No!"

"It's just like the gentleman you are to bring Katie to me before going to your own home . . ."

"Is Father dead?"

"No, but he's not doing well. He's in the City Hospital. I visited with him yesterday. He's been quite eager for you to get home."

"Please excuse me, Goldie. I'll talk with you later. I must see my father at once." He was gone, precluding any further questioning from her. As the carriage bounded out of sight at a frightful speed, Ellis turned to see Cynthia waving after the conveyance, still trying to catch a glimpse of Katie.

At the hospital, Ellis found his father weak, but conscious. "Father! What has happened?"

"It—it was sudden. Like the stab of a knife in my chest."

"What does the doctor say? Does he think you will soon recover?"

"Now that you're here—and married to the girl with the bottomless purse—we'll be fine."

"But I didn't marry Katie, Father."

"You—you *what?*" The mayor's face bleached and he threw his hand to his heart.

"Father, you must try to understand. Katie would

never fit up here. Her faded cotton dress, back-dated shoes, braided hair . . . Just ask Culpepper."

"But you have to marry her, son, however poorly she adjusts!" His eyes pleaded. His breath came short.

"Why, Father?"

"We're in serious trouble, Ellis. We must have Cynthia Goldstein's money or we're bankrupt!"

"You've lost it, old man. We're not exactly poor folks ourselves."

"Listen to me, Ellis. I demand that you listen to reason! If you don't get Goldstein's money immediately, I'll go to prison."

"Your mind has snapped."

"I wish it had. Unfortunately, I've never been more rational. The funds we've been living high on . . . How can I say it and leave you any respect for me, Ellis? I've been embezzling money. Now the city has called for an accounting. Our house, our land, our furniture, our carriages will all go up for public auction to pay the debt I owe. And still it won't cover the amount I've taken over the years. I'll go to prison. And your roof will be the stars above. You'll be fatherless, motherless, and homeless—a nothing, a nobody. No parties. Not even a horse and carriage. Think of it, son."

"No!" A tremor ran the length of Ellis's body. He had never known a life without plenty. "I can't believe it!"

"So now it's up to you, my boy. You've always had Goldstein wrapped around your finger. Promise to return for her niece, but get her money at any cost! You've got to save me! If the niece doesn't fit up here, you can divorce her when we have her aunt's assets in hand. You will do it for your old dad, won't you? It's life—or death—for me."

185

"I'll do it. Just quit worrying and get well."

A relief came over the mayor's pinched face, and he closed his eyes in a restful sleep. The doctor stopped by and smiled. "The invincible mayor will be fine now," he told Ellis. "Your coming has been better than medicine for him."

Now Ellis had no choice; he must take Katie for his bride. He ordered his driver back to Cynthia's house. He would have to be sagacious, watch his words, be convincing. Goldie had spent years in the financial forest avoiding hunters. Crafty, that was the word. He would need to be crafty to get her pelt.

He bounded from the coach toward her gate. She appeared from nowhere and startled him. "You've tortured me long enough, you niece-napper." She laughed as she took his arm and turned him back in the direction of the coach. "Bring my beautiful Katie in and let's play no more hide-and-seek games. Molly has the scones and cider ready—" she stopped. "What's wrong, Ellis?" He stood rooted while she tugged at his arm.

"I'm afraid my own disappointment is greater than yours, Goldie. My bride didn't get to come home with me. She is quite ill. The physician is afraid she may have malaria. They've discovered pollution in the area water. It's not surprising with all those unsanitary cisterns in Greenfield!"

"My precious Katie!"

"She is as lovely as you promised and more. I can hardly wait to get her home and show her off. It was the hardest thing I have ever done to leave her behind."

"Why didn't you stay with her until she was well, Ellis?"

186

"I had a feeling—a sixth sense—that I needed to come home to take care of our financial matters. I do most of Father's bookkeeping, and the servants take advantage of him in my absence." He faked a sigh. "And I was correct . . ."

"I understand, Ellis. Money is such a necessary evil."

"The doctor said it might be several weeks before Katie is able to travel. I shouldn't wish to overtire her."

"The doctor is certain that Katie will recover with no ill effects?"

"Oh, yes. She has a mild case of the disease."

"I hope Lydia and Maynard don't contact it."

"The cisterns are quarantined, and Katie's parents are fine."

They reached the house. "Molly!" ordered Cynthia. "Bring the refreshments for my poor, disappointed nephew." She dropped down onto the wingback sofa and laced her fingers together in her lap. "Now, Ellis, you must tell me every detail of the wedding. Did the wedding dress fit? Did Lydia like it? How did Katie look in it?"

Ellis, anxious to get to the purpose of his visit, nonetheless played along with Cynthia so as not to lose what he hoped to gain. He reined up his impatience and put on a convincing facade. "The wedding was lovely, Goldie. It wasn't like our weddings here, of course, but the simplicity lent elegance. Katie made the most beautiful bride Greenfield has ever witnessed. I overheard some of the town's prominent citizens talking about it.

"I was disturbed that the town was upset—even obsessed—with the murder of one of their church deacons. The distraction was so great that it took some of the attention from our wedding—"

187

"A murder? In Greenfield? Oh, I hope it wasn't someone dear to Lydia. Who was the victim, Ellis?"

"A Mr. Solomon."

"Yes! Katie has mentioned the family in her letters. I believe she was friends to the Solomons' daughter. In fact, I understood that the girl was to be her maid of honor. What was her name?"

"I—I've forgotten—"

"Was it Genevieve?"

"Yes, that's it."

Cynthia's eyebrows knit. "Genevieve . . . No, it was Jennifer!"

"That's it. Jennifer. I knew Genevieve didn't sound right."

"Was Jennifer composed enough to be a part of the wedding party after her father's murder?"

"Oh, yes."

"Have they caught the murderer?"

"He's awaiting trial. The town really has the story blown out of proportion. The tales would be unbelievable even for a stage drama. They have the gangster riding through town on the murdered man's horse, wearing his clothes, and daring the officers to arrest him."

"I'm sorry for the unfortunate distraction, Ellis. People should pick better times to be murdered. But back to the wedding. The dress—?"

"Everyone raved over it."

Goldie smiled, her face swathed in rapture, her eyes dreamy. "What about photographs? You got a good photographer?"

The more Ellis lied, the easier it became. His mind invented lines as fast as his mouth could spit them out.

"I sent Culpepper a day's journey in that wilderness to find a man who knew his business. Portraits are forever. They must endure our children's generation and on down through time."

"You are wise. I will look forward to seeing those portraits. And did Katie's own pastor perform the ceremony?"

"He did."

"What is his name?"

Ellis pretended to search his memory. "I'm not good at remembering names, and I was so excited—"

"The name would be on your marriage certificate."

"I left that with Katie." His fiction left no gaps. "She wanted to keep it near her. It will be some comfort in my absence."

"Of course."

A restlessness, like creeping paralysis, dulled Ellis's mind for listening. He tired of his own oily words. "I'm eager to have her here, but we have a little problem—"

"What is that, Ellis?" She sat at attention.

"About Katie's money . . ."

"Katie doesn't know that I have everything willed to her. For some time now, my health has been deteriorating. The doctor says my heart is weak. He advised me to get my affairs in order. Everything is set up for Katie."

"That's what I want to talk to you about. Katie is uneducated in money matters. She has never had money and would not know how to use it, keep it, or invest it to a good advantage. Why, she might see a poor child and decide to give half her inheritance away! I will not want her bothered with finances. She's such a helpless little thing. Don't you think we should protect her from any stress of mind by transferring the inheritance to me since I will be caring for her for the rest of her life?"

"I think that's a wonderful idea. She might not even know how to go to the garment houses and deal with the hardnosed madams. And with your experience, you would. I should have thought of that myself!"

"Will there be a fund immediately accessible to me for Katie? She has nothing: no clothes, no slippers, no luggage. I wish for her to lack for nothing on our extended honeymoon abroad. I'd like to go ahead and start my purchases, make travel arrangements . . . Father has my own funds tied up with some silly bonds just now."

"There will be no problem. I have more money than I could use in a dozen lifetimes. I've lived these past few years to see that Katie takes my place in society. There's a saying I read on a headstone and I like it: 'To live on in the life of another is never to die.' I like to think I'll never really die as long as Katie is alive to enjoy what I have accumulated."

"You are a generous lady. When can we get the papers drawn up to have those assets put into my name?"

"I'll send word to my lawyer. We'll get the documents signed first thing in the morning. Can you be here by eight o'clock sharp?"

"I'll be here." Ellis, accustomed to sleeping until noon, told himself that this would be worth the inconvenience.

He congratulated himself; he had never known anyone to become a millionaire so easily. At eight o'clock on the morrow, his father would be a debt-free man. They would have their first draw on Goldie's money. They would keep their home, their luxuries, their servants. Life would be smooth again.

With the money, Ellis would have plenty of time to go for Katie (if he found it necessary). To marry her . . . To divorce her. . . .

However, Cynthia Goldstein died in her sleep that night, leaving her will unchanged and irrevocable. Everything she had now belonged to Katie Matterhorn.

Chapter 23

A ROSE OR A ROPE?

omething like a chill gripped Pete. The longer the trial was delayed, the more nervous he became.

"I'm getting itchy feet, boss," he said to Flynn. "Think I might have a touch of cabin fever. When do you think this trial will be over so we can move on?"

"Heard say in town that this is the longest they've ever held a murderer. The constable won't budge until the judge gets back. The town swears on his word."

"Nobody knows when the judge will be back?"

"Nope. He got himself laid up injured. We'll just have to wait it out. You could make yourself useful and chop some wood for our cookstove while we're waiting."

Pete ignored the suggestion. "What would happen if we lit out and left Thomas with no witnesses, Flynn? All the evidence is strong against him. Shouldn't be any doubt in anybody's mind who did the crime."

"We can't do that, Pete. Thomas just might convince them somehow that it was us that did the crime instead of himself. We've got to be here to defend ourselves."

Todd spat a stream of brown juice onto the floor. "My paw always said truth don't need no crutchin', Cuzin Flynn. Th' man would never git by with layin' th' blame on you an' Pete."

"You don't know Thomas," Flynn said. "He's cagey and conniving. He's got a clean look in those eyes that puts words on his side of the chalkboard every time. We don't take chances on getting our necks tangled up in a rope."

"That's what trials are fer, I 'spect, so's no innercent man gits 'is neck hurt bad."

"Have you ever been to a trial, Todd?"

"Nope."

"I was afraid of that."

"Remind yerself that I'm frum th' sticks o' Missoury. An' in them thar hills, we don't go patsyin' to no outside meddlin'. Thar ain't much crime, but what thar be, we eye-fer-eye an' tooth-fer-tooth it, an' th' law never hears 'bout nuthin'. I ain't so sure but ourn ain't th' best way."

"But you're not in Missouri and we're under a different system here."

"Learn me, Cuzin Flynn. Ready me fer this here trial. What will it look like?"

"First, there'll be a judge. All judges are solemn-buckets, poker-faced, *hard* men—"

"Musta all set on rocks when they wuz kids."

Flynn looked blank.

"When I wuz a kid, Grandpap wouldn't let me set on a rock. He said settin' on rocks made abody hard-hearted. Even t'day, I'm soft-hearted as a eggshell. I can't stand to see nuthin' hurt 'er die. But go on learnin' me about th' trial."

194

"When the judge looks at you hard-like, you can't let him get you rattled up. He'll try to weave a web and catch you in it. That's his job. The better he does it, the more money he makes."

"He don't spider round th' witnesses, does he?"

"Depends."

"Depends on what?"

"Lots of things." Belligerence sharpened Flynn's voice. "The law people, they're in cahoots with the judge. They ask a thousand questions. They work together like a team of mules."

"Thet sounds like a good idee to me."

Flynn grimaced. "Sometimes it is; sometimes it isn't. It's bad if they start nit-picking."

"Shouldn't fret no honest person."

"Then there's the jury. There'll be six, maybe twelve, men chosen by the judge and the law officer to hear the case and decide where the fault belongs for the offense. The bad thing is, they get to choose who they want."

"Who will these men be? Us'ns?"

"No, we're witnesses. Jury can't be witnesses, and witnesses can't be jury. The jury is supposed to be unbiased."

"Un what?"

"Not partial to anybody. They'll probably be people who have lived here for a long time. Businessmen, church people."

"Can't see nuthin' faulty with that."

"I hate trials!" Flynn slammed his fist on the table. "Sometimes there's a mixup." His hand went to his throat. He felt around it. "Once when I was a kid, Grandpap made me take a string of beads from around my neck.

He said little boys who put strings around their necks were bound to come to a bad end, likely a hanging."

"Yep, an' he tole me that ifn I slept in th' moonlight, I'd go blind er crazy, an' it never happened. I say ifn yer conscience ain't dirty an' yore truthful, ye ain't got no frets 'bout this here trial."

As the conversation progressed, so did Pete's illness and irritability. "I'm not feeling well, boss."

"Ifn Pete gets a-pukin' an' can't keep nuthin' on his stummick, we can fix 'im up, Flynn," Todd suggested. "Remember th' old yarb doctors in them thar Ozark hills? Warn't nuthin' they couldn't cure up!"

"I try not to remind myself." Flynn wrinkled his nose. "I hated those bitters."

"Grandpap was nigh onto as good as ary yarb doctor in th' hills o' Missoury. An' that's what he pushed on me to be—a doc. But thar warn't enough lucre in it to suit me fancy. I didn't hanker fer no corncob jelly er lambs'-quarter greens fer payback. An' thar wuz too many squawlin' kids to jangle up me nerves."

"What did Grandpap use for stomach ailments, Todd?"

"Th' inner linin' of a cheeken gizzard, chopped up in bits an' made up into tea. Stopped th' crampin' in th' innerds ever' time. Settles th' stummick."

"It's not my stomach," lied Pete, taking on a greenish look. "My head hurts."

"A hot drink will well him o' that, Flynn. Y'know where thar's a peach saplin'? We gotta shave th' bark off'n it an' make up a tea. But ye gotta shave th' bark th' right way. Ifn it's shaved uppards when it ortta be shaved downnerds, Pete'll be like to die frum drinkin' it. Shavin' th' bark upperds can brang pizens frum th' lower parts o' th' body right up into a body's innerds—heart, lungs, an' head—an' could kill abody instantly. But ifn th' bark is scraped downnerds, th' ailment can be driv' down th' legs an' out th' toes thet direction. Them yarb doctors wuz pretty smart."

"We can't be losing Pete before the trial," reminded Flynn. "We need to be very careful about what we give him."

"I'll be fiddling fit in a while," Pete assured. "I'll just rest here easy. I think it's more worriment than sick. Worry just has to pass off by itself."

"Ooze heps worry."

"What's ooze?"

"It's—"

"It's going away now. I'll just be glad when we're in the saddle headed north. This climate doesn't agree with me. It's too hot." Pete, pretending to feel better, went to get himself a drink of water. He was barefoot.

"Always drink outta gourd when you been puny, Pete," instructed Todd. "Water drunk outta gourd is purified water."

"Okay."

"Where's your boots, Pete?" demanded Flynn.

"I hung them up against the wall yonder."

"You *what?*"

"You heard me."

"Tell me you didn't, Pete!"

"I did. Why?"

"Pete! Anybody who hangs their boots against the wall will never live to wear them out!"

Pete said nothing. He jerked on his boots and went

197

outside into the late June sun. It was hot and humid. A black cloud hung in the north. He shook his fist toward it, as if defying it to come closer.

Slowly he turned his hat from front to back, a gesture Flynn said would sometimes reverse one's luck and avoid an unpleasant thing that seemed almost sure to take place.

Then he walked to a rock and sat himself down on it, harboring depression and an unknown fear. He felt he would need to sit on the rock often and become as hard-hearted as possible to face the trial.

Jordan Thomas, an innocent man, would be tried for murder any time now. Fingers of dread reached all the way to Pete's soul. Could he really trust Flynn that they would come out smelling like a rose?

A rose—a rope—a rose—a rope—a rose—a rope—Pete felt himself growing dizzy.

Chapter 24

INSUFFICIENT FUNDS

Attorney Swartz waited at the gate for Ellis Shelby to join him. "Did the madam call for you, too?" he asked.

"Yes. I'm to marry—er, that is, I'm married to her niece."

"The one to whom she has willed her fortune?"

"That's her only niece, sir."

"Lucky boy. Do you realize just how much the madam is worth?"

Ellis licked his lips. "Plenty, I'm sure."

The attorney laughed. "More than that."

"She said she wished to update the papers now that I'm in the family."

"I'll do whatever she wishes. That is my job and she pays me well to perform it."

They walked across the courtyard to the tall-columned porch. Molly answered the summons of the brass knocker.

"Come in," she said and stepped aside. "The madam isn't up yet. You are welcome to wait if you'd like. I'll bring tea."

"Thank you. We'll wait." The attorney and Ellis sat down and conversed in matters of trivia. Attorney Swartz asked after the mayor's health. Ellis was optimistic, cheerful. "Father is made of salt and lined with pepper," he told Mr. Swartz. "He'll be back in the stew in no time." An hour passed and still they waited.

Molly appeared again, her chagrin apparent. "I'm sorry, sirs. Madam never keeps her room this late. I'll slip upstairs and see if I may help her with her toilet." She vanished up the curved staircase.

"The madam is likely going over her figures," suggested the lawyer. "That could take all day."

Molly was gone for some time when they heard her scream. "Help! Come quickly! The madam needs a doctor!"

Both men bolted up the stairs—and both knew when they saw Cynthia Goldstein's stony face on her pillow that she was dead.

"You stay here and I'll go for the doctor," Ellis offered. He left on feet that could not take him from the scene fast enough. It was his first encounter with eternity.

The doctor pronounced the woman dead. She had died sometime during the night, he said. Molly washed the corpse, ordered a casket, and sent a wire to Lydia Matterhorn that her only sister had departed this life.

Ellis stopped the attorney on his way out. "The madam told me exactly how she wanted her finances handled last evening," he said. "I can tell you the changes she wished to make and we can go ahead . . ."

"I'm sorry, Mr. Shelby, but I do not, nor does anyone else, have the authority to alter anything now. The way she left her will is the way it will stand in court. I'm sure that since you are married to her niece, your wife will work with you in the matter. If your wife wishes, it is now her prerogative to put her fortune into your hands. Otherwise, it remains her own. You are a lucky husband, indeed."

"Well, you see, I—I—" Ellis crawfished.

"Where is your wife now?"

"There is a bit of a problem." He cleared his throat. "The truth is, Mr. Swartz—Madam thought her niece and I already married, and I didn't wish to disappoint her. So I let her think that we were. I am to go for the wedding as soon as possible. I had planned to leave today after our meeting with the madam. Miss Matterhorn is quite anxious for my return. But now I will be obliged to stay until after the funeral since Mrs. Goldstein was such a dear family friend and especially fond of my father. After the services, I shall leave immediately to take my bride."

"Miss Matterhorn is unaware that she is the heiress of her aunt's worldly goods. It will be my pleasure to go to Greenfield and inform her of the bequest. I shall go in person to give her any legal counsel that she might need in the matter of the estate."

Ellis saw his chance for an expense-paid trip. "Then I'll just ride along with you, Attorney, if you don't mind. Since both of us must make the lengthy trip, we could certainly keep each other company."

"Certainly! Certainly! The madam wished me to escort her niece back so that she might make an inventory of her inheritance. I would be happy that you, as her husband, have the honor. This was all planned by the madam long in advance of her niece's wedding. Madam thought a lot of her niece."

"As do I, sir."

They parted with a handshake.

Society's hawk, Beverly Judson, heard that Ellis Shelby was home and planned a party to celebrate his coming back single. She sent him an urgent message to come at once, and he hurried to get dressed.

Ellis could not resist a party where drinks were served, even though the body of Cynthia Goldstein lay in state. He merely congratulated himself that he would have no fears of Cynthia walking in unannounced and finding him flirting with his women admirers. He could yield freely to his passions, dance with all the loose girls, give them drunken kisses, pat their bare shoulders.

"I knew you'd come back, darling," Beverly cooed. She waltzed close to Ellis. "You and I need each other."

"What I need is money." Ellis's tongue was thick. "A woman without money holds no attraction for me."

"How much do you need?"

"Enough to pay myself out of some trouble."

"Trouble?" Her big, painted eyes widened. "Has that old bag in the territory got you into a corner, Ellis?"

"Yes, she has," he said. "I had to slip away from her to get back to Father. If I should break my engagement to her now, she would sue me for breach of promise. She is demanding a large sum in exchange for my freedom. I don't love her and I don't want to marry her. Oh, Beverly, darling, what shall I do?" Great crocodile tears wallowed in his eyes.

"I'll get whatever it takes to free you, Ellis. I won't allow that trollop to blackmail you. When do you need this money?"

"Tomorrow."

"Meet me at the bank in the morning. I'll arrange for you to have the funds."

"Do you think you can get enough?"

"I'll get as much as I can. I have a considerable savings."

"How shall I ever pay you back?"

"That won't be hard, Ellis. When shall we be married?"

"As soon as I am out of this mess."

Beverly wheedled and cried for her father to let her withdraw several thousand dollars from her savings and his for Ellis. "It's a small price to see me married to the mayor's son, Father. Just think what prestige it will bring to you. Can't you hear the news? Jack Judson's daughter snagged the mayor's son! We stand to gain much more than we lose!"

She won.

Ellis took the money to his father, who didn't bother to ask where it came from or what strings were attached. He fingered the bills like a starving man would welcome food.

The mayor counted it. "This will stall off our bankruptcy for a few days, Ellis," he said, "but it isn't nearly enough. It's peanuts compared to Katie's fortune. You need to get on down there and marry the girl before some local heathen finds out about the money and gets the jump on you, and we lose Goldstein's precious millions."

"Yes, Father. I am going along with Attorney Swartz. We will be leaving right after the funeral today."

When Ellis left for Greenfield, he posted a loving note to Beverly, informing her that her funds had not been sufficient to get him out of the trouble with Katie. He would, therefore, be obliged to marry the girl he did not love. But he would get a divorce, he promised. "If you can be patient, Beverly darling," the letter ended, "you and I will be married as soon as possible."

Now there would be nothing to throw a hitch in his plans. Katie had the wedding dress. With Cynthia gone, he wouldn't have to worry about portraits or a honeymoon or a write-up for the society page.

"If Katie should wish to switch everything over to my name, you have the proper forms for that, haven't you, Mr. Swartz?" he asked.

"I can do anything she wants done, Mr. Shelby." The attorney smiled. The smile seemed impregnated with some unspoken wisdom.

Chapter 25

THE MOUNTAINEER'S RESCUE

J ennifer Solomon moved from thicket to thicket choosing the reddest of the just-ripening plums for her mother's plum butter. It was Mark's favorite, had been her father's favorite. Her flour sack, almost full, grew heavy.

As she concentrated, reaching for a ruby trophy hidden deep in a prickly bush, she heard a sound that made her whirl around. A glossy-eyed man with an evil grin stumbled toward her.

Frightened, Jennifer dropped the sack of fruit and started to run. Plums rolled away in all directions.

"Ha!" the man leered. "Looky what I've found. A play-pretty!" His breath tattled that he was drunk.

Jennifer, in a frantic effort to get away from the depraved man, turned her ankle on a rock and fell headlong with a painful cry. She sent up a desperate prayer for help as her pursuer lurched toward her.

When she thought her escape impossible, a tall, lanky man with a coonskin cap bounded from one side of the thicket. A cob pipe rode between his teeth, taking the bumps with amazing patience.

"Flynn!" he barked. "Stoppit! You skeered th' poor lamzy most nigh t' death. Git yerself back to th' shack er I'll pernounce Grandpap's secret cusses on you an' turn you to a worser idiot than you be!"

The drunken man's eyes held real terror. "Please don't do that, Cousin Todd! I'll be a good boy!"

"Then git yerself to home!"

The tottering drunkard reeled away as fast as his unsteady legs would carry him.

"Ye awright, missy?" Todd asked.

Jennifer opened her mouth to answer, but her fright erased any words she tried to speak.

"Don't be a-skeered o' me. I'm just an' ole mountain man from Missoury an' I couldn't even hurt a 'possom. I'm powerful sorry thet Flynn skeered ye so bad. He's me cuzin an' he's as clung to 'is bottle as a ninny baby. He's a piteous excuse to be named a man mos' time. I guess I'd'a done left 'im ifn it warn't that I feel obliged to see after him when he gets hisself soused. See, we had th' same grandpap, an' I'm thinkin' Grandpap would expect me to take keer o' me own blood kin." Todd began gathering up the runaway plums and stuffing them back in the sack. "Ye hurt bad?"

Jennifer sat up and winced. "I—I think I just sprained my ankle. Maybe the pain will let up so I can limp home in a few minutes."

"You jest set right thar an' rest yerself. I'll stay close by an' pertect ye as long as ye want. Flynn's a hard man. He set hisself on a rock too much when he was a kid. Now me, I never set on rocks. I favored th' moss better. I'm a softy." He smiled and his eyes smiled, too. "Ye picked

ye some nice marbles here. Even got a few tawleys in th'
bunch. I bound it's fer a pie, ain't it?"

"Mother makes plum butter," offered Jennifer, her
apprehension melting. "My brother especially likes it. And
my father did, too, before—before he was murdered."
Tears budded.

"Aw, missy," Todd hung his head and looked away.
"It pains me to know thet ye are pawless. I got meself
pawless when I was young, too. It's tough. Where do ye
home from here?"

Jennifer told him.

"I don't s'pose this here killin' o' yer paw happens
to be th' one thet got his horse an' duds stole an' th' killer
rode into town with 'em?"

"Yes, sir."

"I ain't worthy fer ye to sir me, missy."

"Our Charley Horse was stolen, and father was slain
by a man named Tomsor."

"I recall Flynn callin' 'is name. Factly, Flynn has to
be a witness at th' trial bein' as he seen it happen."

"The drunk man—saw my father killed?"

"Most nigh did, missy. An' Pete—he's th' one with
th' bad scar acrost his mug—he was thar, too. I'll have
'em both sobered up good an' proper fer th' testifyin' so's
they can do ye a good job." Todd turned his attention back
to her injury. "How's th' leg feelin'?"

Jennifer tried to stand, but couldn't. "I—I hope I
haven't broken my ankle."

"Mind if I feel it, missy? I won't hurt ye. Me ole
Grandpap wuz a doctor of sorts an' he learned me a lots
about hurts an' ails."

She put out her foot, slowly, painfully. Perspiration

beaded on her forehead with the effort. Gently, Todd felt around. "Nope. No broken bones. Jest a grievy bruise. You'll need poultices an' hot soaks an' windin' rags fer awhile. Rest a spell longer—yer pale yet—an' then I'll hep ye to home."

A sigh came uninvited. Jennifer picked up the ball of conversation where they had dropped it. "I'll just be glad when the trial is over. It's—it's been a long wait."

"Cuzin Flynn said th' jedge wuz ailin'."

"Yes, and our constable doesn't trust anyone else. They've lawed together for years and never made an error in judgment. When Mr. Tower visited with us, he said this Tomsor was such a convincing liar, he was afraid anyone with less experience than our own wise judge would be swayed to let the man go free, even with all the evidence against him."

"I'm hopin' it won't be much longer fer yer sake." He pulled at his beard. "Fer mine, too. Pete an' Flynn drinks worser ever day. It seems to be bearin' awful heavy on thar minds."

"I dread it something fierce. I'll be called upon to testify, since I saw the criminal go by our house wearing Father's clothes and riding Charley Horse. I hope I don't faint."

"Can you call back th' murderer's looks?"

"No. I was so frightened, I scarcely looked at him. I—I think I didn't want to see his face. He slowed down and near stopped, but I turned and fled into the house. Then I went into a swoon. I don't remember much about it, but Mr. Tower said I should tell what part I do remember. Mr. Tower believes in giving every man, regardless of how black his crime, a just and fair trial.

He says the most airtight cases have taken strange turns right at the end."

"Flynn says thar ain't no leaks in this case. An' it shore sounds like they got th' dog by th' tail. I done said I'd be standin' around to be in on th' right side. I'd want right to win out ifn it wuz my own grandpap to be hanged."

"We don't know who the murderer is or where he came from. No one from here has ever heard of him. Tomsor. That's an unusual name."

"He lived right in yon house." Todd gave his head a jerk toward the Barnes place.

"He did?" Jennifer shuddered. "I—I'm glad I didn't know that. I wouldn't have slept a wink. As it is, I've slept poorly. And I've had the strangest dreams. I've dreamed twice that the man wearing Father's clothes and riding Charley Horse wasn't the man who really killed Father—"

"Dreams ken be trickish."

"A lot of things don't make sense. The man had my friend's Bible when Mr. Tower arrested him. Bibles and killings don't seem to go together."

"Bibles er sometimes toted by outlaws fer a good omen. They think it'll brang 'um good luck."

"I guess that would explain it. Are—are there other men like Mr. Tomsor up there?"

"Only Flynn an' Pete an' meself. An' ye don't ever have t' worry about 'em harmin' ye. Not s'long as I'm thar. I have me way o' skeerin' 'em spitless, an' I'll do it. They'll be skittish to even look towards yer house when they pass a-goin' to town. Ye saw how I handled Flynn.

"I jest threaten to witch 'em ifn they don't toe up to my bossin'. It's mos' nigh funny. I larned fast thet they wuz superstitious an' I control 'um by it. I ain't got no educatin', but I got enough smarts to know thet most o' thet thar Ozark voodoo is plain ignerant. Me Grandpap b'lieved it ever bit an' me Grandmam b'lieved none o' it— an' she's a'ready outlived him by two bits of a centry an' had a heap more good fortune t' boot.

"Th' way Grandmam put it, it wuz bound to rain on th' jest an' on th' unjest. She allowed bad an' good comes to all of us durin' our visit to earth, an' omens didn't have nary a thing t' do with it. Th' way people lives makes a heap o' difference, she said, cause a body reaps purty much what a body sows, an' ifn ye make yer bed hard, yore th' one t' have t' sleep in it. Thosen's wuz her favorite sayin's.

"I don't put much stock in omens meself, but s'long as I can keep a slobberin' drunkerd in check with my skeers, I'll keep playin' my cards!" He chuckled.

"I—I think I might be able to hobble home now with your help."

"We'll try it. Ifn ye can't make it, I'll go git a horse— er get someone to holp me make a saddle pack."

Jennifer stood. Then leaning heavily on the mountain-ner, she limped home thinking what a spectacle they must make.

Todd doffed his coonskin hat when he met Mrs. Solomon. "Madam, ifn thar's ever anything I ken do fer ye an' yore family in th' sad absence of yer husband, yer to let me know, y-hear? I live right on down th' road a piece to th' ole fallin'-down place yonder. Jest call fer old Todd an' Todd'll come."

"Thank you for gathering up my plums and helping me home, Mr. Todd." Jennifer waved. And it seemed to her that the old mountain man walked away a little straighter, a little taller.

Chapter 26

A LIE IS A LIE

"**G**et up, Pete, and say rabbit for good luck. This is the day."

"What day, boss?" Pete rubbed his eyes. "And why say rabbit?"

"The day of the trial, numbskull. We'll be on our way to a pretty land tomorrow. Better see all of this wilderness you're going to see today."

"I saw all I wanted to see two months ago, boss."

"Careful how you get out of bed, Pete! Right foot first, remember. We've got to do everything just right today. It won't hurt to flirt with Lady Luck extra."

"Yes, boss."

Pete stumbled to the table and picked up his cup.

"Not with the left hand, Pete!" Flynn ranted.

"Sorry."

"I jest hope th' jedge's hair matches his mustache," Todd said. His eyes twinkled. "Different colored means bad luck."

"What time is the trial?" Pete asked.

"It starts at ten o'clock. So hurry."

"Will we walk or ride the horses?"

"Afoot!" The demand came from Todd. "Thar'll be more beasts than thar's hitchin' posts fer."

"I had a bad dream last night."

"Don't tell it until after breakfast, Pete," warned Flynn. "If you tell it before, it might come true. We can't take any chances."

Todd set the pot of gruel on the table. "Now, Cuzin Flynn, mayhap ye'd best remember me what I'm supposed t' tell th' judge t'day."

"I'll be the first to witness," Flynn said. "I'll tell what me and Pete saw. We didn't actually see Thomas strike the man on the head, but we heard the crack of the wood against his skull. We both ran to see what was going on— we were skewering some fish over the fire for a meal— and we saw the man tumble from his horse. Then we saw Thomas ride off real fast—and we didn't see the boy again until he came riding into this place here on a Saturday night. He was on the same black horse. Now get these dates straight, Todd. The murder happened on a Friday, the thirteenth day of May—"

"A mighty unlucky day, Cuzin."

"Yep. We know. Thomas came back the fourteenth day of May after dark. He didn't want anyone seeing him come in with the animal.

"Now why he deliberately got up on Sunday and dressed in the dead man's clothes and went to town, right into the hands of the law, has always been a mystery to me and Pete." He caught Pete's eye. "Maybe Thomas will speak up for himself in that regard."

"And mind you, Todd, the boy is bound to try to lie himself right out of this scrape. I don't think the boy

212

knows how to tell the truth. He may even try to blame the dastardly deed on me and Pete."

"Blood's thicker'n water, Cuzin Flynn. He can blame all he wants, but it'll be his word agin' yourn, an' looks like all th' puddin' is on his side o' th' platter." Todd looked out the window. "A bird jest tried to fly in this house, Flynn. That's *real* bad luck." He looked at Flynn through narrowed eyes.

"Quick! How can we undo the cuss?"

"You throw some salt on th' fire, Flynn. An' you tie a knot in a string, Pete."

Both men jumped to do his bidding. He seemed to enjoy the show.

After breakfast, Pete reminded Flynn of his untold dream. "Can I tell it now, boss?"

"If you must."

"I dreamed about that lizard you told me not to dream about. I dreamed he got himself caught between two big rocks and couldn't get away."

"Just before you went to bed, I told you that you could dream about anything in the world but lizards. And that's the very thing you went and dreamt."

"I told myself not to, but I did anyhow."

"I kinda fergot 'bout th' lizard dream, Flynn. Remember me what it means." Todd looked up.

"It means somebody will betray somebody else."

"Won't be me, boss!"

"You don't think yore own flesh an' blood would Judas ye, do ye, Flynn? I ain't never played false with nobody that was *in th' right.*" Todd came down hard on the stipulation. "So's I don't guess ye got nuthin' to fret over, dream er no dream."

213

"Still, I'm worried." Flynn looked unhappy. "If either of you turncoat me, I'll see you paid back if it's the last thing I do."

They started for town. "Now, we've all three got to butter up that judge and the jury," Flynn reminded, like a teacher giving a review. "Say *Your Honor* and *Gentlemen* real humble-like every time. Is that clear?"

Todd and Pete nodded.

"You sure, Cuzin, that we're the only witnesses?"

"I'm sure."

"Nobody saw it but you'ns?"

"That's all."

"Flynn?"

"Now what is it, Pete?"

"Remember we was going to take that bloody rope that we, er, that Thomas used to tie the man up with, as evidence that we was there and saw the old man? That'll prove we undid the old man and tried to help him back to life."

"They're bound to ask us, Pete, why we didn't report the crime."

"We did. Remember, Flynn? We went all the way into town and when we got back someone had moved the body while we were gone. We had no way of knowing who the man was or where he came from. Remember?"

"Yep, I remember. The rope would make a good score for us with that judge."

"It's bad luck t' go back fer somethin' onct ye've left th' house," reminded Todd gravely.

"Is there a cure if we have to go back, Cousin Todd? That rope is really important. It might mean whether the judge believes our story or not. Cold, hard evidence always influences the law."

"We need it to dangle in front of the jury," added Pete.

"Well, ifn ye gotta go back, ye'd best make a cross here in th' road an' spit on th' cross afore we commence agin'. An' when ye git into th' house, sit yerself on th' floor an' spit three times. Then when ye come along back, come out of th' house backards an' count to ten backards. Then end with amen. That's a lot to remember, but ye daresn't ferget none of it."

"We'll do it all, Todd. Thanks. I don't know what we'd do without you."

Todd waited, laughed.

They started again. A rabbit skittered across their path from left to right.

"Did you see that, Pete?"

"Just a hare, boss."

"But he ran from left to right instead of right to left."

"What does that mean?"

"You don't want to know, Pete."

"No, ye don't want to know," echoed Todd, cutting his eyes toward Pete.

"What can we do to erase that, Todd?" Flynn's shoulders sagged under the weight of the omens.

"Tear yer clothes jest a little."

Both men tore at their shirts.

"Why is it, Todd, that the very day you want everything to go just right, they go just wrong?" Flynn asked.

"I dunno. Ye'd have to upgrave ole Grandpap an' ast him ifn ye wanted to larn thet riddle. I heared him say those exact words many a time."

"But he had Grandmam's disbelieving."

"Mayhap ye have someone disbelievin', too."

Pete put up both hands. "It's not me, boss, Honest."

Flynn made a stab at being cheerful. "This could be good for us. We did all the antidotes; keeps us in good practice for when we go to Colorado tomorrow. I went out about daybust and sat on the hardest rock I could find to get my heart stiffed up to face that judge and jury."

"It shore bothers soft hearts t' see a man condemned to die." Todd thought out loud. "Dyin' is ferever."

"Seein' a man die don't bother me," Flynn said. "But I figure I've got to be tough when the judge starts to ask all those questions just on purpose to get me mixed up. I've got to stand firm against the lies of Thomas and not forget what I'm trying to say. Lots of times witnesses get all rattled up and the judge gets the wrong idea. He gets the notion that they're the guilty ones. That's what I've got to be hard against."

"Jest be honest, Cuzin Flynn," suggested Todd. "I told ye truth don't have no use fer crutches."

"You just say yes, Todd, however mixed up my tongue gets. I've told you who did the crime and how it happened."

Flynn had his fingers crossed in his pocket. Grandpap said if you crossed your fingers when you told a lie, it wouldn't count against your character.

But Grandmam said a lie was a lie.

Chapter 27

WEDDING ARRANGEMENTS

"What's going on here?" Ellis pointed toward the crowd that gathered outside the inn.

"Today is Mr. Solomon's trial," Sadie, the innkeeper's daughter, told him.

"They're just now giving that criminal his just dues?"

"The judge has been out of pocket. But trials don't interest us, do they?" She fluttered her eyelashes and gave him a coy smile. "I'm glad you're back, Ellis."

"I've always wanted to see a kangaroo court in session," Attorney Swartz spoke up. "Who knows? A New York lawyer might learn something of value from these backwoods people. I'm going to slip into a fresh suit and go."

"I have better things to do." Ellis yawned. "I need to try to locate Miss Katie Matterhorn today."

At the mention of Katie's name, Sadie turned back to the books. "Katie will likely be at the trial herself," she said. "She was thick with Mr. Solomon's daughter."

The two men moved into the tearoom. "If you see

Miss Matterhorn before I do, please tell her that I need to talk with her on the matter of Madam Goldstein's will," the attorney said.

"I would like to make my wedding arrangements first, if you don't mind, Mr. Swartz," Ellis said. "Sometimes when a woman comes into money suddenly she gets independent and doesn't feel she needs a man. I shouldn't want to lose my sweetheart now. I'm sure you won't mind giving me a little time."

"Then you'd best make your arrangements immediately." Mr. Swartz was curt. "I need to get back to New York. I have an important case coming up."

Ellis gulped down his tea and left. Directions he picked up along the way led him to the Matterhorn homestead, where Lydia corralled five active children for the Solomon family while they went to trial.

The suitor turned his most gracious charms upon Lydia when she answered his knock. He held his bowler hat in his left hand, extended his right for a handshake. "The favor tells me that you are the beautiful Katie Matterhorn's mother. I'm Ellis Shelby. You do resemble my late friend, Cynthia Goldstein, to a startling degree and I offer my sympathy for your recent loss." He still held her hand; now he kissed it as tears blossomed in Lydia's blue-gray eyes. "Is Katie here, please?"

"No, Katie went with her friend to a trial . . ."

"I must beg your pardon for my hasty departure when I came to Greenfield to claim your daughter's hand previously, Mrs. Matterhorn. It is regretful that I did not get to meet you then, but my father suffered a severe heart seizure and I was summoned home at once."

"I told Katie and Maynard that I was sure some

218

emergency took you away. I knew you wouldn't just disappear without leaving some word—"

"Of course not. But I trust that Katie got the message I instructed Culpepper to leave at the inn for her concerning my father's illness?"

"I'm afraid she didn't." One of the Solomon children became fretful, and Lydia excused herself to sit all five of them at the table with bowls of bread pudding. Ellis heard her instructing the older to see to the needs of the younger. He shifted from foot to foot, resenting the interruption. He disliked children anyhow. To him, they were a bother.

"Is your father doing well now?" Lydia asked when she returned.

"He was well enough that I could leave him to return for Katie. I do hope that we may be married at once, for I have waited quite impatiently for this day. I promised Father I would not be gone any longer than was absolutely necessary."

"It shouldn't take Katie long—"

He shook his head. "I am pained to think that Katie didn't get my message. There's no excuse for my valet's carelessness. That's what one gets for trusting to others. Well, I'll make it up to your daughter, Mrs. Matterhorn. I promised your beloved sister the night she died that I would lovingly care for her niece as long as there is life in my body. She went to her reward with that happy assurance. And I mean to do just that."

"I'm sure you will. My sister thought so much of Katie. I even thought she might leave some legacy to her."

"I have no idea to whom Mrs. Goldstein bequeathed her earthly goods," he lied. "But that's no matter. I plan to care for your Katie both physically and financially so that she shall never have a want."

"And spiritually, I pray. That's the most important. Katie is a wonderful Christian, and she will need a husband to share her faith."

"Surely! You must not worry about anything, Mrs. Matterhorn." He hurried to change the subject. "Katie has the dress her aunt sent?"

"Yes, but it needs some alterations. It's a bit worldly to suit Katie and myself. It would take a couple of days—"

"Oh, I can't bear to wait that long! By all means, she shall wear something else. Anything. I shouldn't think of delaying our marriage for the sake of vanity. She could be married in a print dress for all I care. She'll be as lovely in one attire as another to be sure!"

"Katie has the wedding dress she made with her own hands. She would be much more comfortable in it, though it is quite plain."

"That will be fine."

"I'll press it and have it ready."

"Could you direct me to the minister so that I may assure myself that he will be available for the ceremony later today?"

"The parson may be at the trial," she told him. "Most of the townfolk are." She gave directions to the parsonage. "My husband left just before you came. I'm surprised you did not meet him."

"I passed a man repairing a wagon wheel."

"I hope Maynard had no trouble."

Ellis bowed. "Then you, Mrs. Matterhorn, will be agreeable to the marriage of your daughter and I today?"

"Oh, yes! I'll be only too glad to see the joyful light return to Katie's eyes. She has been so dispirited since you left."

"You will make a lovely mother-in-law." Ellis kissed her hand once more and took his leave.

He found the parson gone from home so he went back to the inn and waited for the trial to end. He hadn't the energy—or the desire—to push through the churning mob to find Katie. There would be time enough for a simple ceremony after the court proceedings. Her mind would be distracted now anyhow.

So Ellis Shelby pulled out a bottle of port wine he had stashed away in his traveling bag and toasted himself with a strong drink to celebrate his upcoming wedding to Katie Matterhorn's wealth. The country girl had no idea at this moment how much she was worth. And if he had his way, she would never know.

Just so Lawyer Swartz didn't ruin everything by informing Katie of her fortune . . .

Chapter 28

GREENFIELD'S TRIAL

The court was to be held on the town square. No building, Mr. Tower said, would hold the people, and he wanted one and all to witness the proceedings of the trial and judgment. This was not only good politics on his part, it was what he considered fair, he said. Benches and cane-bottom chairs had been pulled from nearby businesses to accommodate the crowd.

Jennifer asked Katie to sit with her. Katie wore her favorite dress, the one she had worn the day Jordan snatched her from death—the one she mended so that the rip was hardly noticeable. Lydia insisted she wear a bonnet, but she took it off to fan her face.

The throng gathered, some standing in store doorways, watching and listening. Others moved to the chairs and benches, shading their heads with whatever they could find. It was already getting hot.

Judge Stanley took his seat. Katie was surprised at his gaunt appearance. He must have shed fifty pounds while he was laid up. Once a rotund man, now his eyes were sunken, his cheeks sallow. His shoulders stooped; Katie felt real sympathy for him. She hoped this task wouldn't prove too much for his frail condition. He was a just man, and took no delight in sentencing a man— however guilty—to the noose.

Mr. Tower took a chair to one side of the judge. A blend of weariness and relief showed on his face. This had been a long, drawn-out affair for Greenfield. Everyone would be glad when it was settled and life in the little town returned to normal—if it ever did.

Katie and Jennifer sat near the front with Mrs. Solomon, Mark, Luke, and their wives. "It was so kind of Lydia to offer to keep the children at home," Mrs. Solomon said. Her face, grave and white, showed the strain of the past two months. Mark patted her hand affectionately. "Yes, it was," he agreed. "She's a true friend." Katie looked about for her father, but he had not yet arrived.

Three crude-looking men came into the circle and took their places. Jennifer whispered to Katie, "The tall man— he helped me home when I sprained my ankle. He's nice."

"I don't like the looks of the other two," Katie said in a hushed voice. "Especially the one with the scar on his face. I've seen him before from a distance."

"The balding one is the man who frightened me and caused my fall. He was—drunk. I'm afraid of him. But Mark says they will move on after the trial. I'm glad."

"I am, too."

More parishoners filed in. A mumble of voices rose and fell in a mixture of greetings, opinions, and predictions.

"Whew! It's hot!" The speaker, behind Katie, made

a breeze with his hat. "The day's fever is predicted to go over a hundred."

The silence that claimed Katie's mind was cold; something like a terrible premonition seized her. She wanted to run.

"The court will come to order!" Judge Stanley's voice boomed out with awful authority. "Mr. Tower and myself, we will appoint the jury."

Katie's eyes searched for her father. She had hoped he might be chosen to serve on the jury. He was not there.

The innkeeper and the parson were both selected. Mr. Samuelson from the saddle shop was appointed, too. Others were singled out, all good men, until the panel was complete. They were seated and ready.

"Now, as always, we will have an orderly court here in Greenfield." The judge was stern. "When the murderer is brought in, there will be no uprising or violence. Anyone who gets out of order will be arrested."

When the jailer brought the accused man in, everyone strained to see him except Katie. Her thoughts were elsewhere. Her mind had stolen away across the street, reliving the day she first saw Jordan Thomas. She had only to consult her heart to bring back the details: strong arms that lifted her from the danger, his soothing voice, his kind eyes. . . .

When the defendant sat down, he lowered his head and kept his face averted from curious stares. His disheveled hair, now long and thick, caught Katie's fleeting glance, but brought no recognition of the man.

"Mr. Tower will now give our jury the facts of the case," the judge said. "Go ahead, Mr. Tower."

The lawman stood and the audience sat as if under

a hushed spell. "Gentlemen, on Sunday, the fifteenth day of May, as I performed my duty as the constable of Greenfield, the man sitting before you appeared on Main Street, riding on Matthew Solomon's horse, wearing Matthew Solomon's clothes, and toting a Bible. The community church report from the previous Sunday was in the pocket of the suit he wore. The man told me he was on his way to church—the very church Matthew Solomon deaconed in. He claimed innocence of the crime. I apprehended the man, and as I knew emotions would run rampant in our small community, I took him to Stafford and committed him to the jailer there for safekeeping. That's all, your honor."

"Thank you, Mr. Tower. Now, members of the jury, we will hear from Mr. Mark Solomon, son of the deceased."

Pete's head jerked up, then Flynn's. They looked surprised.

Mark took the stand. "On Friday, the thirteenth day of May, about noon, Your Honor, my father and I were on our way to Montana to help my oldest brother build a cabin. We stopped to prepare ourselves a meal about fifty miles north of here. I left my father with the horses and went to gather firewood. It had rained and much of the wood in the area was wet. It took longer to find dry wood than I anticipated. When I returned, my father had been struck on the head and his horse was gone. He was scarcely conscious, and all he said to me was, 'They took my horse—' and then he reached to his badly cut face and said, 'Scar.' It seemed he was trying to get a message across to me when he spoke that one word. Then he died. I picked up his body and brought it home."

Pete covered the scar on his face with his left hand. The jury nodded and looked solemn.

"Thank you, Mark. Now we'll call for Mr. Flynn, a man who claims to have first-hand information on the murder. You are under oath to tell the truth. Mr. Flynn."

The killer turned in his seat, but Katie watched the man named Flynn. He made a quick cross on his chest, almost imperceptible and probably unnoticed by most of the observers.

"Your Honor, I'm Flynn." He looked at the judge, then at the jury. His eyes were shifty. "On the thirteenth day of May, about noon, we were headed for California to work in the gold mines. There were three of us when we started the day—myself, Pete here," he gestured toward Pete, "and Todd there, sirs. Then the man who committed this terrible killing joined our party about midmorning. He said his name was Thomas, sirs. We supposed him to be an upright citizen. But about mealtime, we stopped to rest, sirs, and he wandered off. We heard a noise and went to investigate. Mr. Thomas, sirs, was riding off as fast as he could and he had left behind a man most nigh dead.

"The injured was bound with this rope—" he held up the dirty piece of hemp. "Your Honor, we untied the poor fellow and tried to help, but when we saw we couldn't, we went into town to report the matter and get a doctor. When we returned, the body was gone. We didn't know his son was with him, but we're glad." He looked toward Pete and Pete nodded. "I say Mr. Thomas, sirs, is guilty of the murder and should be hung by his neck with a rope." He held up the rope once more for effect. "In fact, we'll donate this one if you need it."

"Thank you, Mr. Flynn. Is that all?"

"That's all, Your Honor."

Flynn sat down with a smug air.

"Now Mr. Pete," the judge said.

Pete mimicked Flynn. "Your Honor, my story measures the same as Mr. Flynn's to the inch. I don't know as there's much use to repeat it word for word. Like Flynn said, we didn't actually see the murder, we just saw the horse and rider skittering away."

"Thank you, Mr. Pete. And now you, sir." The judge nodded toward Todd.

"My name's Todd. I never seen ner heared nuthin', Your Honor. I'm jest here t' vouch for Mr. Flynn's words. He's me cuzin. Put me down fer bein' on th' side o' right an' justice, whatever thet side be." Todd sat down abruptly.

"And now we'll call Miss Jennifer Solomon, daughter of the victim, to testify. Miss Solomon—"

Jennifer's voice warbled out, unsteady. "Your Honor, on the night of May fourteenth, which was a Saturday night, just after dark, I heard a horse neigh, and I thought it was Father's horse come home. It sounded so—so natural. Then the next morning, on a Sunday, I went out to pick some flowers to make a wreath for Father's casket.

"I was on the porch when a horse and rider passed our house headed for town at a fast clip. The horse was our Charley Horse, and the rider wore my father's Sunday-go-to-meeting clothes. He slowed down, and I thought he was going to stop. It frightened me so badly that I stumbled into the house and collapsed. I—I don't remember much more, I'm afraid."

"Would you know the rider you saw that morning if

you should see him now, Miss Solomon?" asked the constable.

"I—I don't know."

"Mr. Thomasor, stand up."

The man stood slowly and turned his face toward Jennifer. A look of profound sympathy was written across it.

Katie gasped, felt her head reel, and grappled for the sides of her chair. *Jordan Thomas!*

For one long moment she found her eyes caught by his. When he moved them away, she staggered to her feet; her only thought was to escape this living nightmare.

Chapter 29

UNEXPECTED EVIDENCE

Katie's mind screamed against the shock. *The killer can't be Jordan! He would never harm anyone.* She beat off thoughts of his guilt with mental fists. *No! Not Jordan. He didn't do it!*

On the outskirts of the crowd, Katie dropped onto a bench. Her legs would carry her no farther. Her ears roared with the pressure of racing blood. She tried to think, but her thoughts tangled and knotted and . . . hurt.

She found herself beside a solicitous older gentleman. "Are you all right, miss?" he whispered. "You are as ashen as death!"

"I—I think so."

"Please let me help you to a cooler place. You have gotten too hot . . ." Attorney Swartz led Katie to the sheltered overhang of Boscoe's Hardware Store. He seemed relieved to get her there. "I thought you were going to pass out on me. Was the victim some relation of yours, Miss—what's the name?"

"Matterhorn. Katie Matterhorn, sir. No, I was a

friend of the—that is—oh, sir!" she broke into a wild sob. "I don't believe the accused man is guilty of the murder! He-he would never hurt anyone, sir!"

"Have you reason to believe him innocent?"

Katie's recalcitrant mind reached for some facts, some figures just out of her grasp. She tried to put her thoughts in order. Suddenly she sat up, ridgepole straight. "*When* did the witnesses say that Mr. Solomon was murdered, sir? On what date?"

"On May the thirteenth. A Friday."

"Then Mr. Jordan Thomas can't be guilty, sir." She laughed with the hysterical sort of joy that comes with a revelation. "Jordan Thomas was at my house at noon on May the thirteenth."

"Can you prove that, ma'am?"

"I can prove it. I remember it well. He couldn't have been fifty miles from here!"

"What evidence can you produce to substantiate your statement?"

"I have my calendar marked—it's the last mark I put on it. My mother and father can verify this fact, too, sir. That's two more witnesses that Jordan is innocent!"

Mr. Swartz touched her elbow. "He's being sworn in. They've called for his confession. Let's move in closer so that we can hear what he has to say for himself." He took her arm and helped her up.

"What have you to say in your own defence, Mr. Thomasor?" the lawman asked. "It seems all the evidence is against you."

"Gentlemen of the jury and Honorable Judge," Jordan's voice was low and even; it bore no fear. "The name is not Thomasor, it is Thomas. Jordan Thomas. I

232

won't take much of your time. I'm not afraid to die—for a crime I did do or didn't do. I've made my peace with God. But it so happens that I am guilty of no crime. I did not kill Mr. Matthew Solomon. However, it is my word against all these witnesses." His eyes passed over Flynn and Pete. "And sometimes truth does not win in this life. So do what you must." He sat down. A buzz of anger swept through the restless crowd.

The judge motioned for silence and nodded to the jury, signifying the end of the testimonies, the time for decision.

A man strode to the front—a stranger to the town of Greenfield. The dignity with which he held his broad shoulders, his silvery gray hair, and the clothes he wore gave him clout. Even his manner of walk demanded respect. All eyes were riveted to him.

"Your Honor, there is one witness who has been overlooked, I'm afraid." No words could have been as effective as the pause, timed just right. He looked around at them all. "I am confident that the jury would like all the facts of the case before they make so momentous a decision as falls their lot today.

"I am an attorney from the state of New York. Swartz is the name. Perhaps you have heard of me, though it matters not whether you have or haven't. I came here on other business, but I am now representing Mr. Jordan Thomas, an innocent man. Will you please come forward, Miss Matterhorn?"

The moment seemed suspended, frozen in time. Eternity waited.

Katie moved to the front and stood beside him. She was no longer afraid.

"Gentlemen, all the witnesses seem to agree on the

date and time of the crime: the thirteenth day of May about noon. Is that correct?"

The jury nodded. Mr. Swartz drew the witnesses into the circle of his vision and waited while they gave nods, too.

"Miss Matterhorn has assured me that Mr. Jordan Thomas, the accused, was at her house on May the thirteenth at twelve o'clock noon. Is that correct, Miss Matterhorn?"

"Yes, sir. Jordan Thomas came on that date to return a locket he had found that belonged to me. He had lunch with my family at noon that day. I recall the date well because each day I marked my calendar—in a countdown to my wedding to one Ellis Shelby—and the day Jordan came is the day I stopped counting. . . ." Her eyes met Jordan's. She wrapped all her love in that one look. When he smiled, her heart gave an uncontrollable leap. "Wouldn't it seem, sirs, that Mr. Thomas couldn't be two places at once?"

Flynn gave a nervous cough. Pete half arose from his chair to object, still trying to hide the scar on his face.

"Mr. Thomas, will you please tell the jury how you came to be riding on the victim's horse and wearing his clothes on Sunday, the fifteenth day of May?" Mr. Swartz adjusted his wire-rimmed monocle to see Jordan better.

"If I may take a few minutes of your time, gentlemen, at Mr. Swartz's invitation . . ." The jury settled back to listen.

"First, I must confess that I was with Flynn and Pete when they robbed two of your local residences. Although I refused to participate actively in the thefts—and even tried to release an elderly gentleman whom they tied up—I cast my lot with these unscrupulous men. I even accepted money from them. I planned to use the funds to break away from the outlaws, find an honest job, and then return the money."

"Were you held by these men with any sort of threat, Mr. Thomas?" Mr. Swartz broke in.

"Yes, I was, sir."

"And you are willing to repay the money you received?"

"Every cent of it plus interest, sir."

"Have you the prospects of a job to do this?"

"He does," spoke up Mr. Samuelson. "I've offered him a job."

"You can work out a repayment plan with Mr. Tower, Mr. Thomas. Is that fair enough, Mr. Tower?"

The constable nodded.

"Now to the case at hand, Mr. Thomas."

"On the fifteenth day of May I had planned to go to church, sirs, and meet—Miss Matterhorn there. She had lent me her Bible and I had it with me, planning to return it to her. The two men with whom I lived," he nodded toward Flynn and Pete, "suggested that I ride in on the black horse they said they had bought on Friday to replace one that had been lost in a swollen river. They said the clothes in the saddlebag came with the horse they purchased and that I was welcome to wear them. I followed their suggestions.

"I was apprehended on Main Street by your fine constable, Mr. Tower. He took me to Stafford where I have been in the keeping of a wonderful jailer.

"I wish to offer my apologies to Miss Solomon for the anguish I caused her. Of course, I had no way of knowing that the horse or the clothing belonged to her father. I noticed her discomfort when I passed by on the horse and thought to stop and offer her assistance, but my slowing seemed to frighten her the worse, so I hurried on.

"Thank you for representing me, Attorney Swartz. And thank you, Miss Matterhorn, for your kind efforts to clear me of the crime I did not commit."

Lawyer Swartz turned to the jury. "Sirs, would it not seem incredible for a guilty man to ride into Main Street of your town on the horse of the man he murdered? Would he wear the clothes of the man he killed and walk right into the hands of the law? I think you'd best examine the man with the rope and his friend with the scar on his face. The victim's son tells us that his father tried to identify the man by that scar with his last dying word. There's your best evidence."

Flynn's eyes looked wild. "I just hit him once!" he yelled, shaking his head from side to side. "Pete did the rest."

"Flynn, you said we wouldn't get caught. You said we had an airtight case! You lied to me!"

"And where do you come into the story, mister?" Attorney Swartz turned to Todd.

"That's what I been tryin' to figger meself. I jest want on th' right side. I wadn't even here when th' crime wuz done. I wuz in Missoury. Now I wisht I'd stayed put in Missoury. Me kissin' cuzin turned out to be me killin' cuzin."

The attorney turned to Jordan. "Can you tell us what part this man played in the frame-up, Mr. Thomas?"

"I've never seen the man before today, sir."

"I knew that lizard dream meant something!" spat

236

Flynn. "Todd, you double-crossed me. All that talk about blood being thicker than water, and you go and rat on me."

"I never ratted, Flynn. I told ye frum th' start I'd prop ye up ifn yer story wuz honest. Somebody's got to go back to Missoury an' take keer o' Grandmam. Might as well be me since you don't cotton to 'er way o' livin'. Me—I think she wuz right all time. They's no call fer both o' us hangin'."

"If you gentlemen need an extra rope," Attorney Swartz was saying, "you've been offered one. Seems to me you'll be needing two."

"No!" Pete tried to break and run, but the crowd closed him off while Mr. Tower cuffed him.

Chapter 30

RUNAWAY BRIDE

Jordan sought Katie out after the trial. "Thank you, Miss Matterhorn, for your defense."

She laughed, a light, happy sound. "You saved my life and I saw a chance to save yours."

"I thought you'd be married by now."

"No." Her face glowed. "God worked that out. I'll tell you about it later."

"Did you get your Bible back?"

"Yes, but I didn't know it was you who sent it back."

"The jailer from Stafford was supposed to tell you."

"He gave me the wrong name."

"I knew you would be praying."

"If I had known . . . I would never have gotten off my knees."

"I'm glad you wore that dress today." Love softened his eyes. "It—it gave me courage. It reminded me of all the things you told me about God's ability to put our lives back together. Someday I'll tell you the whole story about seeing that dress hanging on the clothesline. I was with the outlaws then."

Katie, lost in her attention to Jordan and what he was saying, didn't see Ellis Shelby until he had his arm about her thin waist and his hand on her elbow, pushing her away from the crowd, away from Jordan Thomas.

"Come, darling," he said loudly, "I've come to marry you at last!" Then with characteristic scorn, "And you'll never again have to wear a *patched dress* in public!"

She tried to pull away, cast a frantic look toward Jordan. "Please, Ellis, I—"

"Now, sweetheart, I know you are upset with me and you've a right to be. But wait until you have heard my reasons for rushing away. My father suffered a heart seizure and I was called home. The girl at the inn should have given you my message, but your mother said she didn't—the jealous little scullion. I returned to you as soon as my father's health would permit, of course."

"Let go of me, Ellis!"

"You've had a hard day, dear. You should never have been permitted to witness such a crude trial. I'll see that it never happens again. Your nerves are much too delicate."

Jordan moved away. "Jordan—" Katie called, but Ellis placed a hand over her mouth and muffled the call.

"You may be dismissed, please." Ellis surveyed Jordan with cold eyes. "You are upsetting my bride-to-be."

"No, Jordan—" The words were again choked off, only half audible.

"This is my bride and I intend to marry her today. I have made all the necessary arrangements already. Good day, sir."

"I don't wish to marry you, Ellis!" Katie lowered her

head, loathing the scene that Ellis tried to create. But when she looked up, Jordan was gone. She began to weep. "Look what you've done!"

"Cry all you wish, Katie. All women have their tears, whether fake or genuine. I'm accustomed to them. Get it out of your system so you can submit to reason. When you are ready to be reasonable, we will discuss our future in a rational manner. I've already talked with your mother and the parson. We have the ceremony arranged for this afternoon. We must get back to New York at once."

"I could never be happy with you, Ellis. I love someone else."

"That does not surprise me, Katie. Nor does it make me a whit of difference. Love is a relative thing at best—a figment of one's imagination if you will. Women do not understand love at all. The thing that you call love is a mere emotion, a romantic dream. It is not even a prerequisite of a good marriage. Rooted in the soil of economic stability and financial security, a union need never flounder for lack of your so-called love.

"I am not asking you to love me, at least not with your definition of love. In New York, in my culture, you are welcome to keep your individuality. I will never ask of you what you do not wish to contribute to our relationship. And I would request that you give me the same consideration. I will provide for you socially and financially, just as I promised your aunt that I would do—"

"Stop!"

"Surely you wouldn't want to disappoint your aunt, Cynthia Goldstein."

"Aunt Cynthia is dead. Her disappointments are past. She is beyond human appointments. I shall worry about her feelings no more. I am concerned with pleasing my heavenly Father. I shall not want to disappoint Him."

"Your *heavenly* Father? Does your father mean that much to you? I've never met a father that was heavenly yet. Most of them are more like devils—"

"I'm talking about *God.*"

"Oh."

"He will always be my first love."

"So be it. So be it. I have found, Katie, that emotional involvement—whether spiritual or physical—is the cause of all pain and hurts. Remove that and you have none. How would you like a life free from hurting?" Ellis blinked his eyes with a dull sort of excitement. "I can make you comfortable for life. Now, that is my definition of true affection. Come along. Your mother is sensible, and she's happy that I've come for you. Perhaps she can talk some sense into your empty head."

Ellis all but picked Katie up and placed her in Attorney Swartz's carriage, whispered something to the frowning attorney, and then whipped the horses out of town to the Matterhorn cottage.

"You'll fit quite nicely in New York, Katie," he babbled on, ignoring the fact that she was not listening. "There'll never be a dull moment. There'll be balls and parties and clubs to attend. You'll be accepted into society on your aunt's laurels . . ."

Katie focused her eyes on the distant treeline. Her heart went searching for Jordan. He had been exonerated; where would he go now? Thinking that she would be wed to Ellis Shelby today, he would not try to contact her again.

How he must have suffered during those long days

in prison! He had sent the Bible, and thought she knew
he was accused of the crime. But she had not known. Did
he ever wonder if she believed him guilty? No, he would
know that she trusted him, knew he would never commit such a crime. Had he waited, hour after lonely hour,
for her to find him, send him some word, visit him in
prison? If she could just talk to him—

"Katie!"

Her jead jerked up. "Yes?"

"You aren't listening to a word I'm saying!"

"No, I was thinking."

"What were you thinking about?"

She did not answer.

"You were thinking about that wretched man who
was set free awhile ago, weren't you? That shaggy, mangy
cur! I saw you talking to him! I saw that look in your eyes!
But you are never to mention him again! He is not worthy of your thoughts. He's a nothing, a nobody. And I
think he was guilty!"

She lifted her chin. It quivered. "He was not! I know
he wasn't guilty!"

"Look at me, Katie." He raised his hand, and she
thought he would strike her. "What have you and this—
this no-account man got between you?"

"Prayer. An understanding of God's Word. A love
for truth and right."

"Oh, the religious thing." Ellis sweetened. "I thought
it was something else." He tried to pat her arm. "I'm
sorry, Katie. Sometimes I forget. When women become
emotionally disturbed like you have been today at the trial,
they become irrational."

Katie refused any farther discussion. She felt heartsick. She wanted to shut her ears to the squeak of the wheels that took her farther and farther from the man she loved. *Oh, Jordan! How I loved you!*

The minister reined up on his horse just as Ellis and Katie arrived at the Matterhorn residence. "Well, well, we will hate to lose our singer from church, but your mother tells me that you are doing well for yourself, Miss Katie. My congratulations, I'm sure."

Katie said nothing.

"Hurry, Katie, and get dressed," urged Lydia. She looked into Katie's sunken eyes. "I should never have let you go to that horrible trial. It was no place for a young lady. Your nerves have been abused. But all the more reason for you to let Ellis comfort you and take you away to a better life. You will not have to face such taxing circumstances in New York. Soon you will rest."

"But Mother, I can't wear the dress Aunt Cynthia sent. I haven't—altered it yet. Please, can't we wait one more day?"

"It doesn't matter to Ellis about the dress. He says you may wear the one you made yourself; he'll like it just as well. He is a very understanding and humble person, and he realized that it isn't the dress that makes the person. He said so."

Ellis heard and smiled. "You will look beautiful in whatever you choose to be wed in, my dear."

An idea took shape in Katie's mind. She nurtured it.

"It will take awhile for me to prepare for such a special occasion, Mother. I'd like to brush out my hair if I may." She put on a superficial smile that she hoped covered her newly formed plans.

"Take all the time you need, sweetheart," Ellis

offered in a syrupy voice. "Why, it takes the ladies in New York a whole hour just to curl their eyelashes!" He gave Lydia a conspiratorial wink. "It's something I'll have to get accustomed to. I'll wait right here."

"Let me help you, Katie," her mother offered. "Mark came for the children just in time. I told him that we were preparing for the wedding and he was to inform Jennifer."

"I don't need any help, Mother. Please serve Ellis and the parson some of your wonderful teacakes while I make my preparations. I'll call if I need you. I promise."

She went into her room, latched the door securely, crawled out the window, and ran into the woods, determined to find Jordan Thomas on this her wedding day.

Chapter 31

OUTLAWS TO IN-LAWS

Katie made a wide circle. She could see the clothesline with her father's socks hanging by the toes. Lydia had knit another white sock to replace the one that swam down the river. That was about the time Jordan Thomas came into her life . . .

She headed toward town and met her father on the road. Her face was flushed, her hair flying.

"Katie! What's wrong?" He pulled the buggy to a halt and lifted her up beside him, then started for home. "Is your mother ill?"

"Wait, Father! I—I can't go home!"

"Are you all right, child? Did the trial upset you so? You gave a brave testimony in Jordan's defense. I was proud of you! A wheel fell off the buggy on the way in and I came in late—but I'm so glad he was freed. Can you tell me why you are crying?"

"No. I mean, yes." Her eyes implored him to understand. "Please, Father . . ."

Mr. Matterhorn stopped the buggy. "Tell me about it, daughter."

"Oh, Father! Ellis Shelby has come back from New York to marry me. He—he's at our house now insisting that I marry him today. He is waiting. The parson is there, too. But Father, I can't marry Ellis Shelby. I don't love him. I love Jordan Thomas. I just did a wicked thing. I hope that God will forgive me. I pretended to go to my room to dress for my wedding, and I slipped out the window—"

"You don't have to marry Ellis Shelby if you don't wish to, Katie. I should think that he broke the contract himself when he stood you up last time he came."

"I would be the happiest girl in the world to be free from a man who doesn't even know what love is! But I'm afraid I have lost Jordan. Ellis was rude to him. He told Jordan that we were to be married this afternoon—I can't bear it, Father!" She buried her face in her hands to hold back a fresh gush of tears.

Mr. Matterhorn turned the buggy around and headed for town. "In my heart, Katie, I knew that you would lead a miserable life with Ellis Shelby. He isn't our kind. He doesn't love our God. I'm afraid he isn't even a Christian. I've found dishonesty in the man."

"So have I, Father."

"And of all qualities that a real man must have, it is complete honesty."

"Jordan Thomas is honest."

"Yes. Jordan is a true man. I knew it when I first met him. He had an excellent spirit. I like Jordan. There's a chance he'll still be in town somewhere. Maybe we can find him. He was making personal amends to the Solomons when I left."

Jennifer! Katie's heart almost stopped. *What if he*

falls in love with Jennifer?

Back at the square, Attorney Swartz hailed them down. "Miss Katie! I have an important matter I need to discuss with you, please. I promised Mr. Shelby that I wouldn't mention it until he had time to make his wedding arrangements, but I am sure that is accomplished!"

"Yes, it's all behind," Katie said flatly. She cast her eyes about for Jordan. "Father, will you please look for Jordan while I talk with Mr. Swartz?"

"Miss Matterhorn—or is it Shelby already?"

"Matterhorn, sir."

"Your late aunt, Cynthia Goldstein, asked that I convey a message to you on her demise. She has made you her sole heir."

The impact of the proclamation 'did not register on Katie's befuddled mind. "Thank you for bringing me the message, sir."

"Do you realize what that means to you, Miss Matterhorn?"

"That I am to dispose of her personal belongings?"

"No, Miss Matterhorn. It means that all of her wealth is now yours to do with as you choose. And she left you more money than you can spend in a lifetime. That is besides her house, her furniture, her jewels. Their value alone would be the envy of many people who consider themselves rich.

"You are now a very wealthy woman. You could well be worth more than any woman in the territory. I came here to do the paperwork, and if you would like to retain me, I'll be glad to be your advisor in the future and serve you as faithfully as I served your predecessor."

"Yes, please, sir. That is, if it doesn't involve Ellis Shelby."

"No one can involve Ellis Shelby in this matter but yourself. Ellis rode with me here from New York. Otherwise, I have no affinity with the young man at all. I did honor his wishes not to mention the money until he had a chance to talk with you. He advised me that he had marital claims on you."

"He has no claims on me at all, sir. At one time he might have. But any rights that he had were forfeited when he jilted me on his last visit to Greenfield. He has been dishonest about his sudden departure. He left here almost a week before his father suffered his malady. I have a dated letter from my aunt that will discredit his poor excuses for leaving.

"He led my aunt to believe that he was married to me. She sent me a letter of congratulations. I can only surmise that he told her I was too ill to make the trip back with him. She asked after my health, thinking I had malaria. He must have invented quite a story. I can't imagine why he felt it necessary to deceive my aunt."

"Money is a strange taskmaster, miss."

"Did Ellis know of Aunt Cynthia's plans to make me her heir, sir?"

"Yes, he did. He wanted the will changed to his name, and if Mrs. Goldstein had lived another day, he would have succeeded in his plans to usurp her money, stealing it from you."

"Are you suggesting that he had mercenary motives for marrying me today, Mr. Swartz?"

"I'm afraid that's what it amounts to, Miss Matterhorn."

"He certainly cannot love me. And I do not love him. I love the man who was just exonerated of the crime. I would have loved and married Jordan Thomas in poverty as much as I will love him with Aunt Cynthia's fortune. And if the fortune should stand in the way of our love, the fortune would have to go."

"Do you care that much for Mr. Thomas?"

"I love him that much, sir."

Attorney Swartz shook his head. "You are an amazing girl. I wish there were more like you. It would be a better world. Then you won't be moving to New York?"

"It isn't likely, sir. I'm a country girl, and Jordan is a country boy. We would fit poorly with the socialites."

"You are right, Miss Katie."

"Jordan and I," she looked wistful, "that is, if Jordan will have me—will be content here, I'm sure. He's quite fond of my father. And the feeling is mutual."

"Mr. Thomas will be less of a man than I think if he doesn't have you. I'd say he's quite eager to trade outlaws for in-laws!"

"No more eager than I am for him to make the trade, sir!"

"Miss Katie, I feel that you have made a wise choice. I shall set up an account for you here, and you can be assured that I am at your disposal." He bowed and left.

Katie looked about for her father. He was nowhere in sight. The crowd had broken up. Some followed Mr. Tower to the hanging, others went home.

Katie walked slowly across the street and stood by the post that had snagged and torn the moon-shaped rip in her dress. She had found her true love—and lost him— here on Main Street. *But if I go to my grave with only memories,* she told herself, *I can never marry anyone else.*

Tears splashed over the brim of her eyelids, slid down

her cheeks, and dropped onto the patched dress. She was blinded by them. Standing in the same spot, she tried to remember all the details of that beautiful day when love first tugged at her heart. His eyes. His arms. His voice. She closed her eyes to recapture that moment of rapture.

The horse was coming, bucking, snorting. She jumped back. She stumbled. The post caught her dress. He reached for her, pulling her from the path of the animal. Her dress tore . . .

"Katie!" Was it real, or was it a part of the vision? "Katie, your father told me . . ."

She felt herself falling. He caught her in his strong arms and she looked up into his eyes—eyes that told the story of past pain, loneliness, heartache, and included this moment of love—and victory. *This was the other side of Jordan.*

"Katie! Oh, Katie, I love you!" he whispered, and Katie read all his devotion in those words.

He glanced down at her skirt. "You've torn your dress—again."

She laughed. "I know how to patch a torn skirt, remember?"

"So well that one can hardly tell it was ripped." He pulled her lips to his while Mr. Matterhorn, filling a doorway nearby, pretended to look the other direction. "Will you take the job of patching a man's heart?"

"I'll do my best stitching," she promised.

With that, she laid her hand on his chest, looked into his eyes—and went to work.